The Life and Times of Joe St. Roc and Other Tales

By
George Langston Cook

ISBN 978-0-578-02943-6

Table of Contents

The Life and Times of Joe St. Roc

by George Langston Cook

Dedication

This story is dedicated to all suffering with the disease of addiction. Recovering men and women recognize that with honesty comes hope, and with hope all things are possible.

Introduction

I took a two-day seminar on the management of substance abuse programs with Cody Barrett, founder and director of the addiction services department at the hospital that employed me. He gave an assignment to produce a fictitious client database for presentation and discussion of treatment planning on the second day of the class. I created the character of Joe St. Roc to comply with the assignment.

I made Joe out to be a Black Vietnam veteran, a loner who works at the post office in Newark, New Jersey with a heroin addiction. I also gave him a secret, not spoken to anyone until he decides to tell his counselor a story that goes far beyond Vietnam War stories.

As I made my presentation of the client file, the other class participants were amazed at the character I made up. They asked more questions about his life and how his situation worked out, far beyond the class assignment. They thought it would be a good idea if I wrote the whole thing out.

To say the least, I've been busy and never got around to writing the story, but I have kept this character in my mind. I got to think it would make a pretty decent story, maybe even a movie. So over the years I talked about it, did a little research here and there, and received encouragement from my friends and family (along with other writing projects).

Now, more than ten years later, I am ready to tell his whole story. Being unemployed gave me all the time and motivation I needed.

He is an enigma of the times in which he lived. Joseph LeRoque, known as Joe St Roc, a former Marine, and a survivor of hostile actions in Vietnam holds a Purple Heart with one silver and two gold stars, and the Navy Cross. As a father of two that he hasn't seen since their birth, a twenty year veteran of the postal service, heroin addict and Black man, he now needs to find peace from the secrets he keeps deep inside himself.

Any similarity of Joe St. Roc and members of his family to persons either living or deceased is purely coincidental.

Chapter I - Rehab

Joe LeRoque sits passively and inattentively in the middle of a filled classroom at PRIDE, a drug rehabilitation program in East Orange, New Jersey. Most of the faces around him are Black men and women, the rest Puerto Rican, most in their late twenties to their mid forties. He is several years older than most of the others. This is his first day at the program.

It is the first class session of the day following a visit to the detox Joe had just spent the last 5 days in. Detox was rough for Joe since it had been more than twenty five years since he had a day when he did not use heroin. For three days he suffered physically from vomiting, diarrhea, and mentally with the nagging thoughts something terrible would happen to him. He wanted to stay in the bed all day but the nurses and aids woke him up and out of the bed by 7:00 a.m and into session by 9. He hated being where he was.

By the fourth day in the detox unit, Joe started to feel almost human again. He was back to eating most of what was on his plate. The early detox symptoms diminished and he became more attentive during the sessions, but he seemed to distrust the people around him, refused to participate actively in the sessions, and denied he was anything like the other addicts in the program.

A week before Joe was brought into the office of his new supervisor, Max, at the main branch of the Newark Post Office. Joe's heroin habit had finally caught up with him.

"Joe," Max states wryly in a high toned Jersey accent without looking up from a file he held in his hands, "it seems that since you have been here, more than twenty years, and there is no record of the mandatory monthly urinalysis. Do you know why that is?"

"No, sir I don't." replied Joe.

"Well let me tell you why." "The man I replaced was an ex-Marine like you, and he thought it would be best to cover for you because of your service record. In fact," he went on "he passed instructions to follow concerning your personnel file."

Joe responded, "I didn't know anything about that, sir."

"I am sure of that but we have a policy at the Post Office here about drug abuse. We have always had problems with addicts here at the Newark branches."

Joe asked, "Have I ever been late or failed to do my tasks around here sir?"

"No," said Max. "Your record here is spotless, but I wonder how spotless it really is. I wonder that if your old supervisor could get away at hiding twenty years of drug tests, what else can be going on here at this facility."

Joe stood silently, knowing what was bound to come next.

"Mr. LeRoque, you are to be escorted to the staff bathroom by security. You are to submit a sample for drug testing. Do you understand that order?"

"There is no need for that," said Joe. "My sample will be dirty. I use heroin and have been using it since before I came on the postal service."

"Well now." Max slams the file down onto his desk and gives Joe a direct look for the first time. "Well now, you are going to have to do something about it. As of right now I am placing you on extended administrative leave. Your pay will be determined on whether you put yourself in treatment, and show some progress."

"But sir, you don't understand the situation," Joe stammers before being cut off by Max.

"No buts. If you want to continue to work with this organization, you will do this. Either that, or I will see to it that you lose your pension too."

That was a week ago, and Joe had just been escorted from the hospital detox unit to the outpatient drug rehabilitation program across the street. He had a chance to get a brief break where he stood mostly alone, before being summoned in to the first session of the day at the rehab.

Around him the other participants greet each other until the facilitator, Lillian, comes into the room. Joe watches and says nothing. Lillian also watches to see who is participating and who is not. She aims her first question right at the newcomer.

"And what brings you to treatment here, Mr. LeRoque"

Mumbling almost inaudibly Joe responds, speaking slowly in a slight Southern drawl. "I am here because they caught me. I am here because if I did not come, I would lose my post office job, and pension." Then he lifts his voice so that all can feel he is angry about being there. "I am here because that asshole they put in charge of me at the post office wants to make his mark by changing everything. He doesn't know a damn thing," he yells as he pounds his fist into the table in front of him.

All the eyes in the room fell onto him. From in the back somebody, a female voice says "Man you're just in denial that you got a problem. You're just in denial."

Joe turns around as the chorus around him silences itself to what appears to be rage rising up in the newcomer. Joe with raised voice again speaks out. "You don't know a damn thing about me or my situation. All you know is I admitted having using heroin at my job. Besides that you think that I am just like you, that all I do all day long is get high. You are wrong. That is not who I am, it's not what I do!"

Lillian steps in to the fray. "Joe, we are not here to cause you any upset. Just calm down a little and hear what we are talking about. And maybe, if you stick around long enough, you will come to understand what we are talking about here."

Joe said, "I'm gonna be here. My livelihood depends on it, and my pension does too."

"Don't you want to stop using? Hasn't your drug use caused problems in your life?" the chorus of voices chimes in again.

Somebody asked, "Yo man, do you know who your counselor is yet?"

Joe responds more calmly. "Yeah, they told me in the office some guy named George.

The class chorus lets out a unified sigh and the chatter of simultaneous voices begins again.

"Oh man, George will set him straight." "George is just who he needs." "George is the best one here and he seems to know what he is talking about." "That anger stuff won't work with George." "George won't settle for any bullshit."

In the back of his mind Joe begins to ask himself, "Who is this guy named George? Why are all these guys held in awe of him? Can he really be that good or is he just another bullshit recovering joker that wants me to do what he did?"

Again turning his attention to Lillian in the front of the room, he hears a male voice calling his name from the rear side door.

"Joe...Joe LeRoque!"

Joe turns to see a medium height portly shaped Black man with unkempt nappy hair calling his name.

"That's me," said Joe.

"My name is George," the man said. "I will be your counselor. Please come to my office with me."

Joe lifts up from his chair, and exits the room. George greets him with a handshake in the narrow hallway as he is guided into an office near an exit. As Joe sits down, George asks if he prefers the door open or closed. Joe said it did not matter, so George left it slightly ajar.

George starts off. "Tell me something about yourself, Joe."

"What do you want to know?" Joe responds.

"Anything you want to tell me, anything you think is important."

"Well ok", Joe says. "First I don't want to be here and I wouldn't be here if it weren't for the new supervisor on my job at the post office."

George then speaks again. "I heard a new supervisor down there was moved to a post office branch in Fairbanks, Alaska over messing with some decorated war hero. A guy named Max I think they told me was the one that's in Alaska now. Was that you that got messed over?"

"You're kidding me, right? How could you have heard anything like that anyway?" asks Joe.

"I was at the American Legion Post on Elizabeth Avenue the other night and a bunch of guys who work at the Post Office were talking about it. They said the move happened

11

fast, like shortly after he reported that he suspending the guy to the postmaster. I heard his move came down from a very high place. Nobody is talking about that part."

"Yeah it was me that was suspended at the post office by Max," Joe said.

"I have a letter in your file from your EAP that the Postmaster General is saying your job and pension are safe."

"Then my suspension is lifted" Joe queries. "I can go back to work, right?"

"Yes and no. I think whoever moved this guy Max also wants you to finally get it together, so you are still under suspension but with pay during the course of your treatment. Even though our program runs 21-28 days, some people make mistakes that have them here longer. How long you will be here depends entirely on you."

Sitting silently for a moment, stunned about the news, Joe stands and walks to the office door, shuts it and returns to his seat.

"You're a vet George?" Joe asks.

"Yep, Navy, 1970-1974. And you?"

"Yeah, I was a Marine. I did an extended tour in the Nam between 1968 and 1970."

"God bless you that you made it back alive. Is that where you picked up your habit?"

"Something like that but there is a lot more to the story. I got shot up pretty bad over there. They gave me medals, but they really couldn't stop the pain from my injuries. The extended part of my tour was about me trying to end it all, but instead I really got hurt really bad."

"Did they give you morphine?" George asked.

"Yeah, and I got hooked on the shit for the pain. After a while, getting that Southeast Asian black tar opium was a lot easier than finding a corpsman that would keep me in morphine."

"I heard that from quite a few brothers that made it back from the Nam," George interjects. "By the way the folks up there are watching out for you, I wonder, did you get the Medal of Honor for your service?"

"No, a brother gots to die to get that one, but it seems like I got everything else though. In fact since you were Navy you may have heard of me. I got a Silver Star and the Navy Cross back then and they called me Joe St. Roc."

"Wait a minute. You're that Joe?" George asks with a touch of amazement.

"Yeah, that's me. I'm the one."

"No wonder there are people in high places looking out for you. Man, you saved a lot of lives. You are a legend in the Navy and in the Marines."

Again there is a moment of silence, before Joe makes another announcement. "Look George, what I'm gonna tell you I ain't never told anyone. I hope I can trust you, man."

"This is me and you bro. I'm not here to gossip, only to listen, and maybe help you if I can," George reassures Joe.

Okay then, here it goes. Everything that anyone knows about me, it all is based on a lie. My name isn't really Joe LeRoque. My name is James Roach and I was born…."

And the man everyone knew as Joseph LeRoque begins telling a stranger the story of his family, and his life.

Chapter II - Huntsville

It's been two months since Pearl Harbor, and the Army's arsenal in Huntsville has stepped up its production of chemical munitions. Elizabeth Roach had just walked a mile and a half to her home from the road leading to the base where the Army began hiring some locals to work producing weapons for the war.

"I got the job!" Those were the words of Elizabeth, as she burst into the small farmhouse. Her husband, Justice was there with their two teen-aged daughters.

Both Elizabeth and Justice were grandchildren of ex-slaves, living on their small farm in 1942 Madison County, Alabama along with their three children Joseph, Pearl, and Angela. They held on to their forty acre spread though it produced no crops. Unable to afford farm laborers and having too small a family to work it themselves, Justice and Elizabeth both sought and found work off the farm.

Justice's large burly and dark skinned physique belied his gentle nature. A carpenter by trade, and a Baptist by conviction, he applied himself to both, religiously. His large strong hands lent themselves magnificently to his work. Whether building cabinets or an oaken chest, if it was made from wood, Justice had few peers. White folks in the area came often requesting his services, for which he was paid decently in money and in respect.

A proudly religious man, Justice lent his deep baritone voice and humble nature to his church. He sang with the choir, often given a passage in soliloquy because it was said, "his voice made you feel the Lord." He regularly brokered out advice to the members of the small congregation with whatever problems they presented. Next to Pastor Walker, people requested Justice the most.

In her mid thirties, Elizabeth's mulatto skin color and slight build made it possible for her to pass for White if she wanted, but she proudly spoke of her slave heritage. She received more than a primary education while growing up, and she valued it tremendously. When she worked in the homes of White folk, in lieu of monetary compensation she sometimes requested books from their libraries. Her commitment to education showed in her children as she instructed them in reading, writing, and arithmetic at home.

Elizabeth bore her three children by the time she was twenty-two. 18 year old Joseph the oldest child and only son enlisted in the Army following the attack Pearl Harbor. The Army used him for maintenance until he impressed them with his skills. He pursued his father's trade, carpentry, and the Army sent him on building projects on new army training bases popping up all over the country. He planned to marry his sweetheart Lucretia, and live in Montgomery after the war.

Pearl was the oldest daughter, and benefits the most from her mother's teachings. Groomed to be the first member of the family to go to college from her earliest years, Pearl kept to herself and avoided the kinds of attention the other 15 year old girls were getting from the older boys going off to war. The chicken pox as a child left embarrassing scars over her body, and she shied away socially as a result. She made up for her physical and social deficits with a very sharp mind.

Angela was the reason Justice and Elizabeth had no more children. The youngest of the three came after Elizabeth miscarried twice and had a still birth to a set of twins in the four years after Pearl's birth. Angela was the miracle child, the one that was not meant to be.

Angela was special in another way as well. She was overly sensitive and reacted strangely, and the other kids her age teased her a bit. They say she caught the spirit one Sunday at church, and never was able to let it go. She spoke in tongues, often when no one else was around.

To Justice, Angela was his "Baby Girl." She followed him and doted over him, as if he were the most special person on Earth. She'd snuggle on the floor next to his feet when they listened to radio programs, and tried imitating his baritone voice sometimes when she spoke to him. She included him in her games, and he protected her from anything that would cause harm that he could.

"Does that mean I can go away to Tuskegee now? We'll have enough money for me to go?" Pearl asked.

Justice responded in his deep voice, "We were goin' to see you went there regardless of whether your mother got the job at that Army depot or not. With Joseph gone in the Army and wanting to start his own family, it's time we got you prepared for your future now too."

17

"Papa, you and Momma prepared me well already," Pearl replied. "I guess this means I'll be leaving sooner, rather than later."

Justice turns to his wife. "You didn't tell her yet, Mother?"

"No, husband, I wanted to wait until I got back in from the base."

"Tell me, what, Momma, Papa?" Pearl asked.

"I know, I know," Angela said jumping to her feet, and running to a small chest of drawers in the living room. "I read it after I saw Papa Justice put it in here. Let me read it, Momma! Let me read it!"

Justice smiles. "You go on and read it Baby Girl."

"It says bus ticket, Huntsville to Tuskegee, ninety five cents," Angela beams out.

"Yes baby," Elizabeth said. "We bought the ticket yesterday. I did some extra sheets and shirts, and was able to save enough money to get you there, and get you started."

"And I spoke to Pastor Walker about you attending college," Justice continued. "You know he graduated from Tuskegee. He was really impressed at you taking over teaching those Sunday school classes when his wife Biddie went into labor and had little Michael last year. He has written to the school, and you were accepted for whenever we could afford to send you.

"That would be Sunday, after services. We're having the repast here," Momma finished. "So let's show the people at the church, not only are you smart, but you can cook too."

Pearl runs to her mother and gives her a sustained hug, and receives a kiss on the forehead in response. Then she changes places running to her father for the same. Then they all sit down to dinner.

Sunday comes and goes quickly. Following the repast for the congregation Pastor Walker rose to announce the church had taken a collection over the past month and raised forty three dollars to start Pearl off to school. She would still need to work off tuition, books, and room and board by providing services to the school. The next day, Pearl boarded the bus for Tuskegee, and her mother, Elizabeth began working on the base.

Each morning, Justice and Angela would walk together with Elizabeth on her way towards the arsenal, separating only when the school and the depot were in opposite directions. Justice would take his daughter to the school, or with him back to the house where he'd work on whatever projects he was paid for.

In the evenings, Justice would wait for his wife near the intersection of the dirt road leading towards their farm and the main road from the base. There they hugged passionately before meandering slowly towards their home, arm in arm or hand in hand, with Angela jumping out from behind the trees lining the road.

Once home they would enjoy a meal, reading the latest letters from the two eldest, and perhaps they'd perform some service work for the church. Always the evening radio broadcasts included news from the front, a serial or two, and a little dance music that Angela took advantage of by dancing with her father, as her mother looked on laughingly.

And so it went from 1942 into late 1944. To the locals, the sight of the couple walking together inspired talk of the old days when romance ruled. But not everyone seeing the couple came from the locale of Huntsville.

****

"Before you go on Joe, I want to know why these people are important to you," George asks back in the rehab."

"I'm gonna get to that George."

"Well let's pick this up at our next session. I have to get ready for a group now. We'll get together on Thursday, if that's okay with you."

"Thursday would be fine George, and thanks."

Joe walks back to the session room and sits quietly while Lillian continues her session. He stares out the window onto a small flowered courtyard and wonders how much of the truth he could tell the others here in the treatment center.

****

Chapter III - Montgomery

"How can these identical twins be so different?"

Always that is the question people asked of Joseph and James Roach. Born in year after World War II in Montgomery Alabama of Joseph Sr. and Lucretia, Joseph is so outgoing and athletic. He can always be found with friends, running and playing games, while leading the other boys around the neighborhood. He seems to have no interest in academics, though he did well enough in school. Joseph sang in the youth choir at church as singing was a family trait.

On the other hand James was introverted and cerebral, hardly the description that applied to nine-year old black boys in the 1955 South. He seemed more comfortable reading the scriptures, or singing in the youth choir of the Dexter Avenue Baptist Church. The new young pastor there, Reverend King, often commented about young James' dedication to the word of God.

Joseph Sr. makes his living by fixing up the homes of genteel society. A master carpenter by trade, he is known far and wide not only for his craft, but for his deep religious convictions as well. He is a quiet but firm man, as strong in his belief that the Lord will provide for those who keep faith in his word, as he is with a hammer, chisel, and nails.

Joseph sings. He possesses a beautifully baritone singing voice, and leads the adult gospel choir at the church. He is a peaceful man whose only punishment to his children is a stern gaze, and those soft deep tones that can chill you to the bone. No one could truthfully prove any ill in his character or behavior save himself, for he believes he could always give more to the Lord.

Lucretia, known informally as Lu, offers her services as a maid or a cook, whatever the well to do need of her. She seems just as comfortable on her knees scrubbing floors belonging to others as she is standing for hours to prepare elegant meals for special occasions. When not caring for the households of others, she becomes the loving wife and mother. Her youngest offspring, Gail and Margie are always nearby once she got home from work.

As with her husband, Lu participates very actively with the church. She teaches a Bible study class for the children each Sunday, and often sings solo in front of the full choir. Her voice, best described as a colorfully, rich alto that brings tears of joy, and frees people from their pain depending on the occasion. If she decided to use this gift to sing Jazz or the Blues, fame would be her constant companion, but her faith and conviction to serve the Lord receives the full attention of the gifts bestowed upon her. She is a pillar of strength to the other ladies in the church and of her surrounding neighborhood. She gives advice freely and offers support for rightly decisions.

Individually and in harmony, Joseph and Lucretia could easily catch the envy in Cleveland Court, except that their gifts and contributions lifted the spiritual nature of others. They wanted for nothing materially. They lived modestly in a rented small meagerly furnished wood frame home.

The outside plumbing lent it the same character dominating other homes in their section, while the small garden provided extra vegetables for the table. They gladly gave away what they had to others in greater need. Somehow Lu made everyone comfortable in their home, and there always seemed to be enough food to feed everyone, and for a guest or two.

Joseph's two younger sisters also lived with the family, as they had since the death of their parents before the war ended. One of them, Angela, was incapacitated, touched by the voices only she heard. They say Angela had not been the same since she saw her father and mother, Justice and Elizabeth lynched by some white soldiers in the woods near the base at Huntsville.

Elizabeth caught the eye of some white soldiers from up North. When they saw her along the road with this burly Black man walking with her, they thought they had to defend her honor. They mobbed Justice as Elizabeth stood by screaming. Justice fought back the best he could but he was outnumbered and soon overpowered.

Angela walked upon the scene from where she played out among the trees as the soldiers were setting the fire under her now hanged and desecrated father. She heard the screams of her mother but could not see her, as Elizabeth had been dragged into the brush and taken advantage of by several of the soldiers after finding out she was not a white woman. Then there was silence coming from where her mother had been screaming moments before. Angela began to cry out, "how could you all do that to Justice. How could you?"

No one knew for sure whether they accosted Angela in any way, but neighbors and locals came running at the sign of smoke along the road, where the found who they believe to be Justice hanging from a tree, and Elizabeth, clothes ripped off, cut and bleeding from mortal wounds. That was eleven years ago.

Now, Angela spent most of the day, sitting on the porch in the front of the house in a granny rocker. Still in her young twenties, she would rock in the chair like she was an old woman, occasionally talking seeming to herself, and always about her father whom she called by name. "Justice demands you do this" or "Justice is gonna come back and straighten this mess out, just wait and see." Everyone left her alone to herself when she started with Justice, except that sometimes James would sit and listen to what she was saying about the grandfather he never knew.

Joseph's other sister, Pearl, taught in a Negro school. She was homely and unremarkable physically, but she was smart beyond compare, almost frightening so. A few years older than Angela, she was away at school when her parents were lynched. She being the oldest girl, and younger than her brother, it fell upon her to end her studies to care for her sister. When she returned from the college, she was carrying a child though she was unmarried. So Pearl gathered up the household memories, some pictures, some books, and Angela and moved to Montgomery first. After the end of the war, the family was reunited as Joseph and his new wife, Lucretia moved into town. Angela, Pearl and her young son moved into the same house with her brother's family.

The twins James and Joseph, so it seems acted so differently, but like their parents worked very well in concert. At the age of nine, James creates new things to do from his own imagination, and Joseph just goes out to do them. They lack the desire to be mischievous, and both are obedient, thoughtful, and sincere. It's just that Joseph has a touch of daring, and is in many ways like his idol Jackie Robinson. He wants to be the first and the best at everything. He plays hard, but fairly to those he competes against. If he knows he can beat someone in a race, he'll make it close until the end. He is careful of not hurting the feelings of others by the way he performs. He is also not one to bite his tongue. When he sees something wrong, he speaks about it.

James is the one that seems to know what to do about what Joseph finds unfair. He stands aside alone, appearing aloof to the world around him but observes everything. He keeps his thoughts his thoughts to himself, unlike his twin, until he devises a plan to deal with what situation he has to. James doesn't compete, for winning and losing races is unimportant to him. He enjoys the thrill he gets just from running.

During the summer months, Joseph and James play together while their parents work, along with Len, their slightly older cousin and Pearl's only child. During the school year, Pearl insures they keep ahead in their studies.

They laugh a lot together, as if they share a secret between them. They are as good as being friends as they are with being brothers.

The senior Joseph also enjoys taking his sons out of town into the woodlands and teaches them how to set traps and ambushes for quail and rabbit. Each fall, he takes his sons out for a week, and by their seventh birthday, they were doing more than retrieving the small game he shot. Each had their own .22's which they were on their way to being crack shots by their ninth year. James seemed out of place to others when he would begin to bag game first. His adeptness on the hunt belied his more cerebral persona.

When Joseph and Lucretia arrive home from work after being apart all day, the twins show their individualities and go their separate ways. Joseph picks up one of his father's tools and attempts to master it by working on an old log in the back yard. James on the other hand, chooses to read passages with his mother preparing the Sunday school lesson, and listen to gospel songs with his parents.

Joseph Sr. would split his time evenly between the two, giving Joseph some handy man tips, or singing along with James. He always left them with a manly hug and words of encouragement. It was always a "Hey, that's pretty good", or a "You can do it". His voice carried enough weight for either of his sons to believe what he said and to have confidence in themselves, within this microcosm of the Black community of this Southern city in the late fall of 1955.

****

"So it seems you come from a loving church family, Joe. Do you still practice your faith?" George asks

"No. I mean my family was a loving family but I don't go to church anymore."

If I am hearing you right, two generations of your family, three including you when you were younger actively participated in church. You may need to think about what makes you not attend church services.

"I think fear more than anything else that makes me stay away."

"I think it's good you broke it down to a feeling. Maybe you are starting to learn a little something here," George says.

"I think I always knew it was fear", Joe said.

"That may be so, but I would like you to explain that to me at our next session. How does next Monday afternoon sound?"

"It's okay."

"Joe, just make sure you bring that paperwork I gave you to complete."

"Okay G."

****

Chapter IV - For Justice

"It all started on one day, the first of December. Ms. Parks was too tired to stand, too tired to move from her seat when that white man made that fuss that got her pulled off the bus and arrested." This is how Pearl, Joseph Sr.'s sister started speaking about the boycott. Joseph easily persuades his family to go along with it, especially after Angela began talking about Justice as other members of the neighborhood walked by the house. She confused the people who did not know about her. They thought she spoke of the concept when in her mind she was talking about her father.

She would begin as the bus boycott supporters approached the house on their way to get a ride to work. "Justice won't do nobody any harm. All they want to do is destroy Justice. Justice wants only what right for family. He stood there trying to defend the weak. I saw them set Justice aflame and cut him up. They took parts of his body and fed some to their dogs. Yes, I saw them do it. And here they are trying to do it again."

"If Justice was here," she'd carry on "they would have to admit they are wrong for what they're trying to do to us. They can't look Justice in the eye for the fear of seeing their own soul burning like they burned him up."

Sometimes when she spoke of Justice, Angela jumped and prayed as if the Spirit held her in rapture. Other times she broke down, choked up with tears, and swelled with pain.

Her brother would start a gospel song, Lucretia would follow, and the neighbors would join in.

These were the days of the boycott. Each morning before the crowd of folk headed out on their walk to work, Angela sat in her chair on the porch, unable to join, but always willing to lend her spirit to the cause. And for most of the many people within ear of her voice, she extorted a yearning for the social justice in the South. That was the message they took from her each day on their walk to work.

Joseph and Lucretia began having problems finding work because of Angela's daily encouragement to the crowds. She was becoming almost as well known as Ms. Parks and Pastor King, despite the fact many of them folk began thinking she was a bit touched in the head. White folk told Joseph maybe he should not bring her outside each morning. They told Lucretia maybe they could find some task for her to do, if only she could find something inside her house for Angela to do. Joseph and Lucretia took this hardship in stride, only confiding it with the pastor of their church. They never gave in.

And the twins would sit and marvel at their Aunt Angela. They listened to her stories about the kind of man Justice was, how good and how strong he was. She always spoke in a manner of adoration for her father, not unlike any young girl enamored by the loving nature of that singularly important man in their life. James, especially, found great enthusiasm when his aunt spoke of his grandfather, a man he never knew. James yearned to have the same character so vividly described by such a loving, lonely daughter.

At one Wednesday night service, late in the spring of 1956, one of the ministers asked the congregation made up of mostly the young people of the church; "Do you know why no one is catching the bus in town? Do you know why we must travel this road?" A long moment of deafening silence hung over the group. Then there was a creaking sound of someone standing up from his pew seat. And in a quiet yet powerful voice, young nine year old Joseph said, "We are walking in peace for Justice." There was another silence, and Joseph began singing "We Shall Overcome."

Everyone there would have expected Joseph to say the words, and for James to do the singing, but Joseph did them both. He quoted a verse from Proverbs. "He who pursues justice and kindness will find life and honor," he said, as the congregation transfixed by the seemingly sudden change of personality listened intently to his quietly dynamic voice, just as they would have listened to his father. On that day, Joseph began leading a youth ministry. He kept that position at the church throughout the duration of the boycott, and for the five years after, when he and his family moved up north to Birmingham.

Joseph Roach was on his way to fame in the ministry, with his brother James his greatest supporter. James' attitude towards his brother's success came from him not needing to compete, and being more willing to be cooperative. Besides, James acquired his own fame by assisting the pastor with his rounds through the neighborhood. He listened hard to the elders especially whenever talk of how to accomplish a goal came up. He truly understood strategy, though no one knew for sure how well.

And this too, continued until the family moved to Birmingham late in the year of 1961.

****

"Joe. You mean you marched with Dr. King?"

"Yeah, I did. So did everyone else in my family."

"But now you're not active in the church, and you don't participate in any politics whatsoever. What happened?"

Chapter V - Birmingham

When work became a little hard to find for Joseph Sr. in and around the Montgomery area after the time of the 1960 elections, he made a decision to move the family to Birmingham late in the following Spring… up on "The Hill". The family supported the decision to move. There was plenty need for a good carpenter. They found a small church on 16th Street in Birmingham to be to their liking, as well as a modest house they could afford with slightly more room, and indoor plumbing.

The nine moved in together, with Joseph, James, and Len slept in the same room, Angela and Pearl shared space, and Gail and Margie, now age nine and ten respectively, slept in their own room. Everyone enjoyed the new surroundings and made friends quickly.

A tenser atmosphere sat on Birmingham in the early 60's than did Montgomery during the bus boycott. People were dying there. Killings and bombings punctuated the normally dull news. Bull Connor made life harder on Black folk than it had to be. And Angela would sit in the front of the house, and talk about Justice, as the first two years passed almost uneventfully for the family.

James and Joseph begin to get the same notoriety they had in Montgomery. Now about 17 years old, Joseph would visit other Birmingham Black churches, speaking to the teenagers, and teaching them about the times they were going through. James would help the pastor with his rounds, planning meetings, and contributing to an overall effort.

In August, both young men accompanied their pastor and a small congregation from the church to Washington, DC. There they met up with their old pastor for a large demonstration on the Mall in front of the Lincoln Monument. Thousands upon thousands were there. And in that singular moment of history, when Rev. Dr. Martin Luther King Jr. delivered his "I have a Dream" speech, Joseph and James were there with him on the podium.

For most, talk of that happening would fill their mouths for years to come, except that a few weeks later, at home in Birmingham, "it" happened.

It was early on the third Sunday in September, more than an hour before services were to begin at the church. Gail and Margie were preparing themselves for choir in the church basement and decided to go outside for a few minutes to see if one of their friends was on her way. Not more than a minute after their getting out to the street, the explosion occurred.

Gail and Margie's lives were spared, as the basement they had just left was devastated. Though they were unhurt, four of their girlfriends perished in the disaster, crushed by the weight the rubble. Gail and Margie saw their friends' lifeless bodies stacked together life beef in a butcher shop. They screamed and cried out loud along with the other survivors, but there seemed to be no comforting them.

And Margie started talking to herself just like her aunt Angela talks about Justice.

The bombing of the 16th Street Church outraged all of Black Birmingham. The news of the cowardly attack reached everywhere. Fearing for retribution instead of seeking to protect, Bull Connors cracked down hard on the Black community and issued a curfew in those neighborhoods. He worked up his pals on and off the police force inciting the police riot that followed. The pastors of the four Black churches were arrested for investigation for the bombing of the church. The rampaging police dragged Black men off the street and used dogs and fire hoses on groups of teenagers seeking only to pray together at the memorial service the next day.

And then a passerby, strange to the neighborhood saw Angela on the porch surrounded by some of the locals, and heard her yelling and screaming about Justice, saying how much she loved Justice, and how much she needed Justice in her life right now. It took only an hour afterwards for a squad of police aided by their sympathizers to storm onto the porch, and to drag the bewildered Angela kicking and screaming from the house for inciting a riot.

Joseph Sr. saw this as he came outside to find out what the commotion was all about. He ran towards the police to explain his sister's problem only to be knocked down and stomped on by the sympathizers.

Young Joseph came running from down the street and tried to cover his badly beaten father with his body. A gunshot rang out, and blood oozed from a wound somewhere on young Joseph's body, as he lay motionless on the street.

Lucretia screamed from just inside the door. Gail and Margie hid in Pearl's room in the back of the house with Len. Someone threw a fire bomb into one of the windows, and the house became engulfed in fire.

James was in a nearby home when he heard all the noise. He looked out of a window and saw the flames enveloping his home. He tried to get outside, but the family he visited with restrained him. Yelling overheard from the street saying there was one more of the bunch at that Washington march to find let it be known James was also a target of the mob. Protecting him from harm became the only concern of these family friends.

They hid James as his home burned to the ground. No one came out of the front of the house, and the police dragged the beaten father and son duo into a waiting paddy wagon.

At nightfall, the family hiding James told him Birmingham was not a place where he could ever be safe again, and that they had friends in Memphis he would be able to live with until the atmosphere in Birmingham changed.

They told James when he gets to Memphis he would have to change his name because Bull Connor had friends all across the South. They gave him a little money they had saved, and a bus ticket to Memphis. They promised James they would send him any word about his family they could find. They ferried James out of town to Linton after dark where he was to board a bus that made local stops in small towns on the way to Memphis.

Before boarding that midnight bus, James filed away the kindness he received and the pain delivered by others that day. He issued a quiet question to the Almighty. "Why?"

And that was the last Birmingham saw or heard of James Roach, as he assumed the name and identity of Joseph LeRoque.

****

"You really hit me with a lot today, Joe. Let's relax now before you go on okay?"

"Sure. In fact can we continue this tomorrow? I haven't talked about this before, I mean ever. I must trust you a lot George."

"Sure, it's almost time fore feelings group anyway? Go share what you are feeling in the group. You still don't need to say why you feel that way, but you do need to express the feelings. Then we can pick this up tomorrow or Wednesday."

"Okay, I'll give it a shot. Later."

And Joe gets up out of his seat, and leaves the office.

Chapter VI - Exile

The bus ride from Birmingham to Memphis with local stops takes a little more than six hours. Sitting in the rear, still worried sick about his family, James, tried getting a little sleep when the bus stopped forty five minutes out of Linton. The bus driver left the bus and opened the baggage compartment on the right side of the bus, removing the bag he saw the lone Black teenage put underneath the carriage. Getting back on the bus, he walks to the back and wakes only Joseph.

"Get up nigga. Get up and get off my bus. I ain't havin' no Black nigga kids on my bus. Now get off you."

James thought he had to be dreaming until the driver grabbed him and roughly pulled him towards the exit, and pushed him off the bus to the side of the road.

"And ya betta' listen to me boy. All this out here is Klan country, and this is a Klan roadway. If they catch you, and I hope they do, they'll hang yo' black butt good and proper. Get off the damn road fo I'm sho gonna tell 'em where I let you off. When you here them dogs barkin', they'll be comin' afta you, boy."

As the bus door closes and it pulls off, James hears cheers and laughter. He had no idea where he was. It was dark and there were thick woods nearby the road. He knew that it was best that he stay out of sight, so he left the roadside for the safety of the forest.

James reckoned that although he had a few sandwiches and a little money they would run out if he squandered them. He also decided to move slowly through the woods at night and stay hidden during the day, heeding the warning of the bus driver about the Klan. He figured he would still move towards Memphis to look up his neighbor's friends, and that it should take only a few days.

A month goes by, then two, and James is still out in the woods. Weeks had passed since he last saw his baggage, money, or the sandwiches he tried so hard not to squander. Every time he approached an area of population, he'd hear sounds of discord and complaints about freedom riders. Fearing they were still looking for him, James would dash back into the cover of the deep forest.

During this journey from exile into isolation, James thought a lot about what he should do for the rest of his life. He felt uncomfortable hiding out and doing what he must to get food and stay alive. Maybe, he would reason, he should turn himself in. Then he would think of the people who ferried him to safety and what would happen to them. He would think of what happened to his family, too. Though he wanted to come out of hiding, he also knew he wanted to be safe, and to do that he had to avoid the limelight at all cost. He knew no one could ever know who he really was. He decided to change his name to Joseph LeRoque.

James felt a similarity between himself and a story he read about a French healer named LeRoque who had to stay hidden and lived in exile. The ruler of the land at the time was jealous of LeRoque's power to heal and popularity with the townsfolk. When LeRoque came out of hiding, he was jailed and then executed. James thought he had to stay in hiding to avoid the same kind of fate at the hands of Bull Connor sympathizers.

He took the name Joe to honor his father and his brother. He knew Joe LeRoque had to be a different person than James Roach.

For food Joe would lay snares for small game, rabbits and muskrats. If he wandered past an isolated farm, he'd lay in wait for an opportunity to steal a chicken and something growing. Although he was raised in the city, Joe knew how to catch and butcher small game from hunting with his father. He learned how to kill and prepare poultry from watching his Aunt Angela wring necks and pluck feathers to prepare them for cooking.

At about nine weeks out from Birmingham, Joe hears the lament of gospel music coming from a nearby community. Feeling safer by its warm and familiar refrains, he heads towards it and the voices of the people making that sound. As he moved close enough to hear conversations, Joe discovers that someone had shot and killed the president, the President of the United States.

Joe's thinking became erratic. He thought if they could kill the president, they could get anyone. He thought maybe because of all the things he was trying to do for Black people Bull Connor's people that were behind it.

In fact, he was sure of it, just as they were behind the destruction of the only thing that meant something to him, his family. So Joe stayed hidden in the woods and hills between Birmingham and Memphis for another six months, running from any sound of barking dogs and people.

Joe made it to Memphis in the early summer of 1964. Joe, now use to living in the wild made a home for himself under a train trestle crossing the Mississippi River and above a dirt road along the river, instead of looking up the friends of his Birmingham neighbors.

It was there in July that a sanitation worker, Bill Davis, passing by in his pick-up notices him, and on a daily basis tries to strike up a conversation with the 18 year old.

"Young man, what are you doing out here all alone? What is your name and where you from?"

Initially, Joe would retreat further up the embankment and into the bush, never responding to Bill. He didn't know if he could trust this stranger; that even though he was Black that he may still be one of the Bull's boys. But Bill kept coming back every morning and evening, checking in one the young man on his way to and from work. Then one day after about a week and a half, Joe came down alongside the road when Bill's truck approached.

When Bill asked this time, the youth gave the name of Joe LeRoque, and beyond that wasn't very forth coming about his past. After a few more weeks of Bill coming around every day and bringing a little food, Joe told Bill he was orphaned some time ago, and that his family had lived up in mountains north and east of Memphis. He also had said he did not believe he had any living relatives.

Bill was pretty good at sizing up people and thought Joe was not a bad guy. He offered Joe a job helping out on his garbage route which Joe accepted. Knowing Joe did not have a place to live, Bill invited him to room in his home with he and his family.

Joe was a bit reluctant about the offer after nearly a year living without a roof overhead. Catching some kind of bug with a nasty cough changed his mind, as the sickness weakened him so badly he thought it could have easily nearly laid him out for good.

Bill brought Joe to his home, and his family helped to clean him up and nurse him back to health. His young daughter, Lizzy, even took a liking to Joe, and poured over him whenever she could.

Lizzy was a few years younger than Joe, and he thought she would be about the age of his sister Margie. He thought she was cute too, but at the same time too young for him.

A few weeks later after Joe had gotten back on his feet, Bill used his influence with his supervisor to help Joe get a sanitation job with the city. Giving Bill's address as his, Joe applied for the low paying job.

Before the city accepted him to sweep the streets though, Joe had to get a social security card and register for the draft. Without any documents to support him, Joe wondered whether any one would believe him or his story.

Bill accompanied Joe to the building housing the Social Security office. Before he allowed Joe to ask for what he needed, Bill introduced himself first to a supervisor, and from that point Joe had no problem getting a card and number. Once having the card he was able to register for the draft. Joe paid no attention to what Bill said to the supervisor. And was just happy Bill was able to help him out.

Joe avoided as much closeness as he could with anyone, and remained intensely guarded about his past. He kept his own space in the roomy attic that he made relatively comfortable, and went to work on schedule. He never socialized outside of Bill's family.

While working with the city, Joe lived with Bill and his family, and contributed to family finances and attended most of their functions, except for anything that had to do with church or singing. Joe would not even go into a church. He believed if he went into a church, he would not be able to restrain himself, and would draw unwanted attention, or that someone may recognize him. The last thing Joe wanted to do was to endanger this new family, especially Lizzy.

Bill never pressured Joe to attend services, as he himself lived in a manner as if he were agnostic about such matters. What did seem to confuse Bill was that Joe avoided any discussion about Dr. King, voting, or civil rights, but Bill did not let that get between the growing friendship he shared with Joe. Besides, the way Lizzy possessed as much of Joe's time as she could, he figured it might develop into a family situation after a while.

When Joe wasn't alone or at work, Lizzy found some way to be around him. She thought he was a handsome man, fine was the word she used, with his now six foot tall, lean, dark skinned frame. She always told her friends he looked like he stepped off the pages of Jet, and didn't act like anyone else she ever met. She said even though he was a street sweeper, she could imagine being very happy with him.

Over the next few years, Joe stayed with Bill and his family. Every once in a while though, he would take a few days off spending them in the Shelby forest north of town snaring rabbits, turkeys, and other small game, something he continued from his time on the road from Birmingham and in his youth with his father and brother.

In the late spring of 1967, Lizzy graduated from high school. She had grown into a very attractive young lady, nicely developed, brown complexioned, witty, and happy to be around Joe. She knew he was keeping some awful secret inside, but thought he it was that he had a girlfriend or a baby somewhere that he would be going to meet when he said he spent time hunting in the park. She didn't care though, because all she wanted was for Joe to be her man.

Though he tried to avoid it, Joe found himself warming up to her as well, closer than he had let himself get to anyone in the last four years. On two occasions, Joe got close to telling Lizzy about who he was and what he had been through, but begged off.

Late one night, Joe found himself again awakened by memories of the events he had hidden from for years. Sweating from head to toe, he got up out of bed and went downstairs to the porch, and sat on a swinging bench. Still breathing hard and shaking, Joe was startled when Lizzy sat down next to him covered by her nightgown and a robe.

"What's wrong Joe?" she asked.

Joe could not answer, still upset by his nightmare. Lizzy took his hand and squeezed it gently, then reached over and kissed him quickly on the lips. He froze, he had never kissed her or been kissed since Birmingham. Then she kissed him again, this time a little longer, and with more passion. A tear welled up in his eyes as he wrapped his arms around her, and sobs escaped from his chest.

Joe was as strong as Lizzy had imagined he was all along, and she loved his strength. And there on the porch bench, in the early morning hours Lizzy gave herself to Joe, body and soul, and he gave himself to her.

Bill and his wife Betty watched from the darkened window of their bedroom for a few minutes, then they looked at each other and smiled. They quietly pulled down the shade, closed their bedroom door that they opened when Lizzy left her room, and together shared in the passions that seemed to infect the house that night.

At breakfast, Joe and Lizzy announced they wanted to marry. Bill and Betty gave a blessing for the planned union with letting on about their view from the window. Joe said he was happier than he had been in years. He said before the wedding though, he would tell all about himself and his family. Bill told Joe to hold it until later, and that his secrets could keep until after the wedding takes place.

For about a month, Joe and Lizzy made plans for the wedding to happen in the early spring of the next year. But early in July she came to Joe crying. Though they had been together only the one time, the first for both of them, she had missed, and she knew she had to be pregnant.

A few days later after discussing the situation with Bill and Betty, Joe and Liz went to a Justice of the Peace and took the vows as man and wife. And they could not be happier, but Joe's world came crashing in on him again.

It started off with the word "Greetings," the telegraph Joe received a few days after his marriage and short honeymoon. He had received a draft notice to report for induction into the Army.

Because so many young Black men were being drafted, Joe figured his recent marriage would not be able to get him a deferment. Weighing his options, Joe decided to enlist with the Marines instead the Army.

So, in the middle of July 1967, 21 year old Joe left for Paris Island for basic training, and a new chapter in his life unfolded.

Chapter VII: Stateside

Basic seemed liked just that for Joe. He naturally had the discipline and the physicality the drill instructors worked so hard to instill in the other recruits. He took the hardships without complaint. He possessed ability to traverse the obstacle courses and his desire to help his platoon succeed made his sergeant smile. He excelled in all aspects of the Island's physical rigors.

Though having always using handmade traps and snares with his hunting, and though he had not held a rifle since hunting with his father as a youth, Joe obtained marksman status as a rifleman without the need for extra training. His maturity shined above all others in his platoon.

The company commander and the gunnery sergeant made repeated attempts to promote him to squad leadership positions prior to completing the course of basic, but Joe still fearing the limelight would cause problems he did not want, he always found a way to sabotage any elevation. Even without the position, his leadership within his squad and throughout his basic training company was unquestionable.

During basic, Joe kept in regular contact with Lizzy and Bill. Religiously he wrote her daily, and called every weekend. He thought of little more than just getting back to them. He also never got around of telling his secret to them, and he promised himself he was going to live to do that.

After 12 weeks of basic, the Marines Corps shipped Joe out to four months advanced training, where he upgraded his marksman status to expert. He was unable to block an advancement to lance corporal after that.

Early in February 1968, with his training nearly complete, Joe received orders to join the Marine for duty in the Republic of Vietnam in early April.

Joe had three weeks home before he had to go to the Nam. Lizzy was very angry about the situation because she was real close to having the baby. At the same time, her father Bill was having a tough time because of a looming strike against the city by the sanitation workers, and was a quieter than his usual outgoing self.

Joe tried on a few occasions to tell Liz about himself, but when he tried to begin, she would tell him to listen to the heartbeat of the baby she was carrying. She told him whatever it is he had to say, save it until he came home safely from Vietnam, to save it for their child.

At the beginning of his last week home in Memphis, Joe heard an important visitor was also coming back to Memphis to help the striking sanitation workers demonstrate for better wages, Dr. King. After not having any contact and discussion dealing with civil rights or religion in years, Joe summoned up the courage to call his old pastor on the phone one time before leaving for his duty in Vietnam.

Early on that Thursday evening after his father in law Bill had left for a strike rally, Joe picked up the telephone and called the motel and room advertised as the place Dr. King would stay and gave the name of James Roach.

Hearing the response to the announcement of his name over the phone encouraged Joe to go even further. He set up an appointment through an aide to come visit early the next day before he had to report back to camp. And just about then, all hell broke loose.

Joe heard sounds of background commotion and yelling through the phone erupting at the motel. The words "get a doctor, he's been shot" made Joe's blood run cold. He has been here before. He called Lizzy and held her close to him, crying and screaming about what he heard on the phone.

Outside more yelling and screaming rang out as the news of Dr. King being shot hit the news, and it seemed to Joe, that another riot just like the one in Birmingham was about to break out in Memphis. All through the night sirens and shouts disturbed any chance for peace.

Also Bill had not yet come home from a rally that was to take place an hour before the killing. Joe was worried but Lizzy was more of a concern. In the anxiety of the times, her water broke, and her labor began a few weeks earlier than anyone expected.

Betty called a midwife she knew from the neighborhood because getting her daughter to a hospital with all hell breaking loose in Memphis was out of the question that night. A little before sunrise, just as Bill was getting home, the first of a set of healthy twin boys came into the world.

The twins surprised everyone. Bill and Betty's families have never bore twins. The boys weighed in at a little more than six pounds each, and had good size.

When the midwife finally allowed Joe into the room, he looked with joy and amazement at his wife and sons. Lizzy smiled weakly at him, and said a dream told her she would bear twins. She said she even picked out names for them. "The oldest" she said "would have to be a junior and the other should have a name from the Bible. What do you think of the name James?"

Joe looked directly into his wife's eyes, and for a moment did not know what to say. He fell to his knees and moved closer, and in a barely audible voice, he professed his love for her. "James" he said "would be fine. I could not have chosen better myself.

Chapter VIII - The Nam

On Monday, after five days of cuddling with his wife and beaming with joy with his in-laws, Joe left Memphis. He sent postcards from San Diego, Honolulu, and then Manilla. By Friday, he landed at the airfield in DaNang.

He and some of the other replacements were herded onto trucks and moved on to a temporary posting. In three weeks, Joe was in his first engagement with the enemy at a small hamlet just south of the DMZ, a place named Dai Do.

Joe saw limited action in the three day battle due to a small arms flesh wound in his right side that he incurred on the first day. He was evacuated back to the Navy hospital DaNang for recuperation.

During the time he was in the hospital two Navy nurses gave him more attention than his wound required. One of them seemed especially enamored by his physique. He woke up one night with her sitting at his bedside, with a funny smile on her face.

"Time for your...bath...Marine" she said as she pulled the cordon around his bed. She then sponged him down, paying particular attention to Joe's private parts.

"Stop that", he said. "Stop that". "What are you doing to me?" he said pushing her away. "I'm a married man, and I love my wife."

"What are you, some kind of saint?" she asked laughingly. This is how we heal you, big boys here. I know what I'm doing. You will feel better in a minute," she said as she came back to stroke him. Before she left she forced a kiss on him, one that turned him cold.

Joe's torment went on during his three week hospital stay. He valiantly held off the nurses who continually referred to him teasingly as the saint.

Joe had never thought White women officers acted like that, that they would do what they did to him. He knew that it was something he would always be embarrassed to talk about. He also felt how he eventually gave in to their sexual advances would make it hard for him to ever look Lizzy in the eye, again.

Joe received a Purple Heart for his gunshot wound in Dai Do while at the hospital. The two nurses at the hospital that gave him the inordinate amount of attention also put in to his record a recommendation for an award for meritorious service for actions not involving a hostile enemy, the Navy and Marine Corps Medal.

After healing for three weeks and being placed in the personnel pool for another three, Joe was attached to a platoon within another division. The nickname given to him by the nurses, "the Saint", stuck to him with his Marine Corp buddies though they were not sure why he was called that.

The next time Joe saw combat, he was sent to the Dien Ban district of Quang Nam Province as part of a clear and sweep operation. In his first taste of battle, Joe was unsure of himself. He knew what was expected of him, but the live fire fighting took his breath away. With comrades being hit all around him, time did not allow him to notice if he hit someone back. That changed in Bo Bien in August.

The division and other units came under heavy fire, and Charlie was making some headway from their fortified positions in the village. Joe was in the rifle company squad with the forward observer, attempting to pick out targets for Marine mortar fire. He felt a slight breeze blow from behind him, then heard a loud noise, before finding himself propelled ten feet away from where he had been kneeling. His face felt warm and wet, and his vision blurred, but he was able to pick out four North Vietnamese regulars closing in on an unconscious officer that lead the scouting party. Joe reached for his piece and dropped three out of the four, then withstood a charge from the remaining soldier.

A brief wrestling match followed. Joe weakened from the blast and concussion, rolled on the ground in the direction of his fallen squad members, taking the much smaller adversary with him. Joe held him, with both arms wrapped around the soldier's body in a bear hug. The man yelled out as to alert others to his location when Joe forced his foe onto an unsheathed bayonet.

The look of horror on the man's face gave way to darkness. That was the last thing Joe remembered as he passed out after the scuffle.

When he woke up, a corpsman was applying bandages to his head. "Man, no wonder they call you the saint. What you did out there was like crazy man considering the gash you got from that mortar round. Nasty little bump on the noggin too, brother man. You gotta be more careful out there."

Joe felt a little dull for more than an hour, but he gathered his wits when the fighting in the village spilled out into the surrounding jungle. Charlie seemed to be coming from everywhere. It was chaotic, as it seemed that more than one regular company occupied the small hamlet, and they were threatening to overrun all of the Marine positions.

Joe picked up his piece and reported to the first gunny he saw. "I can still shoot," he said. "What do you want me to do?"

The sergeant beckoned Joe to follow, and they crawled through thick underbrush surrounded by low canopied trees near a clearing close to the village. Joe took a high position in the tree line, and set up a sniper's nest. The sergeant stayed low dropping satchel charges into a poorly hidden VC tunnel. Joe shot several enemy troops when they tried to escape their hiding place through a secondary exit of the tunnel. Then Joe moved his location to avoid being detected, and continued to knock down Charlie.

Stragglers from the squad and other forward units joined Joe and the sergeant as they continued the firefight. They gradually moved their positions closer and closer to the village.

Occasional small arms fire punctuated tense moments of silence as the company moved up and several platoons occupied supporting positions on the fringe of Bo Bien. Though the action was intense, the Marines fought their way into the village just before nightfall.

Once the Marines moved in, Charlie hid himself from open view. Joe, the sergeant and two more squads occupied two huts on the edge of the hamlet, where they had a good view down through the center of the village.

Now joined by a second lieutenant, the squad was given orders to bed down for the night before sweeping through the rest of the village at daybreak. Joe stood watch as the sun set, and was relieved by another lance corporal as evening turned to night.

Joe was sound asleep when the corporal on watch yelled the words "grenades incoming." The next thing Joe remembered was that sentry throwing himself onto a grenade that had landed by him, absorbing the brunt of the concussion charge with his body, saving Joe and his squad in the hut.

Stunned for a moment, and his head still throbbing from the noise, Joe picked his rifle up and placed himself just inside the hut's doorway. The lieutenant shot up a flare, and the light revealed Charlie coming up from tunnels in large numbers at the far end of a compound, and already beginning to overrun the Marine position in the second hut.

Joe slung his rifle up and begins firing at regular NVA units nearing the hut he was in. Joined by other members of the squad at his position, Joe got up, exchanged his weapon for a BAR, and with one Marine lugging the stand and another, the ammo, they set up in the open between the two Marine held positions, and cut loose. Minutes felt like hours as he and the two other Marines held the point, while the squads in the huts were able to move the wounded men and the hero back to more fortified Marine positions just outside the village in the jungle. Two other squads came up and the firefight continued for about an hour and a half. Then all was quiet again.

All through the night, Joe could not stop thinking that this may be his last moments alive. He thought about how close he had come earlier that day of not seeing Lizzy and his sons again. He thought to himself that he must have been crazy to jump out of the hut like that, then realized he wasn't thinking at all when he did it. He just reacted. That worried him so much, he hardly realized that he was bleeding again.

At sunrise, when two platoons moved up, Joe was sent back to see a corpsman. "Look brother man. You gots to be mo' careful out there. They don't give brothers the Medal of Honor unless they die as a hero, and you ain't got to be no hero. All you gotta do is survive. Remember you a Marine. You ain't here to die for your country. You here to make sho' the other fellow dies for his. You got it, brother."

"Yeah, I got it." Joe said. "Fix me up and let me get back to the squad. I'm okay. I ain't hurting."

"That's the morphine I had to give you yesterday before you went out with the gunny. You may need some more before too long the way you are bruising up."

"If that's what you think, okay, but I'm not laying up in no hospital. I can walk. I can shoot. So clear me, or I'll treat you like I treat Charlie."

The corpsman complied but warned Joe to take it easy on the stuff, that someone else won't be so good to him. He also told him some other things to remember.

"Look brother, I don't know where you come from, but I know about this stuff coming from Newark. If you feel sick, like you gotta cold you can't kick, you need some more of this."

"If you can't find somebody to give it too you, drink a lot of whiskey, but that's kind of dangerous out here in the bush. The best thing you can do is to smoke that black tar the brothers serving with Army units keep. When you get home the only thing that will work is dope."

Joe listened but did not really pay attention to the warnings the corpsman gave him. Instead he put the small morphine packages in his pack, and then rejoined the action in and around "Dodge City".

Joe fought with his squad in operations throughout Quang Nam and Quang Tri Provinces over the next nine months.

If he got hurt, he always refused evacuation to a hospital, always saying "I can walk, I can shoot," as an excuse.

He received several injuries that sent him to the corpsman who in turn kept him supplied with morphine. Joe thought it was something that would go away once he "got better." He never did, and he began smoking the opium during quiet moments on base.

On extended sweeps where he wasn't injured, he found other blacks in nearby operating Army units that had come from cities like Detroit, New York, Chicago, and Philadelphia with the same problem he did. They knew what was really going on about the morphine habit than Joe did.

Though drug use was considered intolerable with the Marine Corp, Joe's habit was addressed by a wink and a nod by officers in units he operated with and around. Based on their decision to do nothing to him, Joe began to express openly about being sick and hurting from his injuries. Eventually, even officers of various Marine units wanting to use his skills supplied him with all the opium he wanted.

Joe gained battlefield notoriety in places like the Da Krong and A Shau Valley, and DaNang. On more than one occasion, his tracking and trapping skills learned on the road from Birmingham and honed in the Shelby Forest, helped him uncover booby-trapped paths, and sniff out Viet Cong ambushes. Then his nickname "the Saint" grew into a persona admired as courageous sometimes above and beyond the call of duty.

Joe had other reasons for his acts of bravery. At times during sweeps, he had nightmares of his parents and relatives of how they were brutalized. He thought about the reach of people like Bull Connor. And these nightmares and thoughts just made him so mad he had to take it out on someone. That someone was Charlie.

Also Joe began finally to understand he was addicted to morphine and opium, and that he was embarrassed by it. He didn't think it would be right to return to his lovely wife and children feeling guilty about his habit, and not wanting to stop it. Then there was the issue of him being adulterous. It became all the more reason not to survive.

Meanwhile, back in Memphis, Lizzy and her family became more and more worried about Joe. From the time he was involved in the action at Bo Bien, his letters arrived less frequent and were becoming vague. She knew of his injuries because he always sent home the medals, while not discussing what they were for. He never wrote about his buddies, and rarely did he respond to her concerns about his safety.

By February 1969, he had stopped writing all together, and never explained why. And though she tried, she was unable to get the Marine Corps to do more than insure that she received her monthly allotment, 90 percent of everything Joe made as a Marine.

Chapter IX - The Legend

At the end of March 1969, Joe was told most of his squad and platoon was returning stateside. He was also told he would be ordered to take a special position, as an observer and advisor with the brigade of South Korean ROK Marines. Joe was told he would be stationed with this unit during their enmeshment with other Marine battalions during major operations in Quang Nam province.

Maybe it was the Marine Corps' way of dealing with their embarrassment, hoping their "Saint" would not have to come back at all.

ROK Marines had a reputation they upheld whenever they moved into a district. They would send a patrol out to capture two or more VC. They would then systematically torture their captives over a period of hours, letting one live, barely, then freeing him to go back to their units. Usually after hearing ROK Marines were in an area, either the VC became more vicious, or they left an area, and the ROK Marines did not seem to care which.

In-bedded with the ROK Marines, Joe operated like he was one of them. Joe was quick to catch on to their brutal methods of dealing with the VC. The ROK Marines seemed amazed that Joe had no tail like they were lead to believe, and that he was unusually gifted in tracking down enemy squad members, while avoiding capture.

In July 1969, while on a "seek, observe, and clear" mission, the brigade Joe was assigned to became the assault point seeking out VC units guilty of a series of ferocious hit and run actions. Late on the night of the new moon, Joe operating away from the main force with two other ROK Marines, slipped out of camp and took positions in the canopy two klics from the fence. There they waited throughout the night to catch Charlie in a pincer movement between them and the fence.

Just before sunrise, a rustling sound in the jungle floor beneath them indicated a much large contingent of Regulars moving towards the camp than expected. Unable to signal the base, Joe and his triad waited and followed the troops until Charlie was near the perimeter of the jungle, a hundred fifty yards or so from the barbed wire fence surrounding the base.

When the VC started setting up mortar and rocket positions, Joe and his team struck. Successful at taking the VC by surprise initially, Joe's team destroyed attempts at a surprise attack on the base. Charlie retreating from the firefight at the base focused their attention on the three-man attack team, Joe and the two ROK Marines.

The first member of the team to fall was hit while trying to change firing positions. When he fell out of the tree, the VC seeing he was Korean decapitated him, as an act of retaliation to how the Korean Marines fought.

Joe was the second member hit. After taking down what appeared to have been an officer, the tree Joe was in was set ablaze. Though Joe escaped the flames, he was knocked down from behind with a rifle butt to the head.

He awoke bound and gagged kneeling surrounded by fifteen or more Viet Cong. One having a machete hit him with the blade broadside, and another kicked him in the face. He stayed conscious somehow for twenty minutes of intense brutality, where it seemed the idea was that he suffers without dying.

At first stoned from smoking the opium, the pain did not bother him, but the longer the beating went on, the more he felt the urge to cry.

A small group of the VC chatted in a circle, before coming towards Joe with their weapons drawn. A single round from a hand gun hit Joe in the right side of his chest near his shoulder. They began beating him with unmercifully with the butts of their rifle. No part of his body was safe.

In broken English one came through the crowd of smallish Asian faces saying "you want be like ROK, now you ROK. We treat you like ROK. You be ROK now."

All the voices then mimicked the phrase "you ROK now, you ROK now," while continuing the beating.

Joe was found still bound, blindfolded, and stripped naked in the afternoon three days later by a patrol from the camp. He had pungee sticks driven deep into the back of his thighs, and had bruises all over his body. Chunks of flesh were missing from his arms and buttocks. His breathing was very shallow. His face bled badly with blood caked up in his hair.

The patrol that found him said they would have missed them if they had not heard the muffled whimpers mixed in with the words "me ROK now, me ROK now.

"Man I don't know what he could have gone through, but he is damn sure a Marine. He's our own saint, our own ROK."

No longer able to resist, the Marines evacuated Joe by chopper to DaNang, then aboard the Forrestal, from where he was flown to Subic Bay, to Honolulu, and on to San Diego where they expected him to die within days from the severity of his wounds.

He lay unconscious in his hospital bed for three weeks. When he awoke there was a throbbing pain all over his body, and a handwritten letter on the night stand from Richard Nixon, the President of the United States." It read:

Son:

I am sorry you were still unconscious when I came to San Diego. I heard of the sacrifice you made in the face of an enemy in far superior numbers, giving up your body only to insure the safety of your comrades in arms. And we, the American people appreciate what you have done. We will always be in your debt.

As of now, I'm going to do for you something that has never been done. In your name I am issuing a special executive order, guaranteeing lifetime federal employment for you.

You will be retired from active military service with the rank of a master sergeant, and full VA disability benefits.

And I hope you don't mind the trinket I left under your pillow.

God bless you. And God bless America.

RMN

Under the pillow, Joe found a medal, the second highest medal a Marine can get for action against the enemy, the Navy Cross.

He moaned out in pain, and a nurse came in the room.

"Mr. LeRoque!!! Everyone thought you would die. You lost a lot of blood and took a terrible beating. Are you hurting? Let me get you something for the pain."

All Joe could find to say were the words, "me ROK now Saint ROK now."

Chapter X - Rehab

It has now been two weeks since Joe first started telling George about how he got to be who he was and where he was. George had a million questions to ask as Joe left some things quite vague.

"Joe, you say you loved Lizzy. Then how could you leave her to take care of two kids by herself? You let twenty something years go by without making contact with her or the boys. Please make that make sense to me."

"Look. I don't know if I can. I just thought she would be better off without someone always looking for dope. And I got myself to believe they would all be in danger if somehow those people in Birmingham were still looking for me. And she is getting every penny of the disability benefits."

"Do they even know where you are?"

"I tried not to give any hint to where I am, or that I am even alive. I've been more than tempted to go down there a few times, but I always get off the bus in Philadelphia and come back."

"How do you know how she is doing?"

"I don't. I just hope she and the boys are okay."

"And you never thought of going down to Birmingham to check out what happened to your family?"

At first snapping back an answer Joe said "Man, George don't you know they still burning churches in the South." Then in a swift change of heart "Oh, forget that smack. Sure, I want to know what happened, if they got justice. I'm just scared to."

"How did you end up here in Newark?"

"Remember I told you the corpsman said to me he learned about dope growing up here. And when I was recuperating in San Diego, I ran into another Marine, a Jewish guy. He said outside of Asia and Europe, Newark has the best quality dope in the world. What's funny about that is that he's not from here, but knew all about the drug scene. And I parlayed that guarantee to a fair paying job at the Pee Oh."

"Joe, you told me a lot about you, your life and how you feel about things."

"Yeah. You're easy to trust," Joe responded.

"So what is it going to take for you to open up in the group sessions?"

"I participate, George"

"Sure you do, but you can up the ante."

"What do you mean?"

"Maybe you can stop telling the group they don't understand, and tell them about the things they don't understand."

"George, I told you a lot about me and you say this is all confidential right?"

"Isn't everybody still calling you Joe?"

"Well, yes."

"And talking to me about it has been good for you, right?"

"Yes to that too."

"Maybe it's time to let it all out. You know sharing is like vomit. It feels bad keeping it in, it feels nasty coming up, but once it's out, oh what a relief."

"You're funny George."

"Maybe I am, but then again maybe it's time for you to begin trusting just a bit more. You know what I say about sharing. Tell what you can. If you are trying too hard to keep it in, then it's time for it to come out. Stop forcing stuff. If the pain is too great when you are trying to make it come out, it's not ready to come out. What are you really concerned about that prevents you from sharing now anyway?"

"I've always wondered about what I hear at the program here, that addiction runs in families. It makes me concerned about what may have happened to my boys."

"Yeah, they teach that the root to drug abuse may be hereditary, but I will never teach you that. Everybody prefers to feel good to feeling bad. It's just that in some places it is easier to find a drug to make you feel good than to do the work or go through the pain."

"That sounds good, but I'd like to know for sure, but just like when I first got here, I'm afraid. I'm afraid they will reject me; that they don't want to know me. I keep hearing those young brothers here say how their fathers weren't there for them when they were growing up, and blaming that on their drug use."

"Well you had your father growing up, and you still ended up using drugs too. Right? And if so, what does that mean to you? And if you are so worried, why not reach out to them?"

"George I gotta think about that."

"Okay go back to session, and you can get with me on what you came up with on Thursday. Is that alright with you?"

"Yeah, that will work."

"Make sure the other assignments I gave you are done too. I want you to give some thought to having a family conference here too."

"By the way George, will it be too much trouble if I started by telling everyone my real name is James."

"All of life is your choice. Anything is okay as long as you can deal with the consequences."

"Call me James then, George."

"Ok James, go back to session."

Entering the classroom from the back door, James walked in on a session called Podium that was already in progress. Tom, another counselor was facilitating the session.

"Joe," he said. Come up here and answer the questions at the podium.

"Okay Tom, but I'd like to make a statement to everyone first.

James walked to the front of the room. Though he had been opening up some he still kept a lot inside. Reaching the podium, he read through the questions. This is the third such session since being in treatment.

"I want to start off by saying hi everyone. You all have come to know me as Joe the mad man from the post office."

Everyone chuckled briefly at him poking fun of his hard exterior. Then the all got quiet as he ruffled the papers in front of him, and tears flowed down his cheeks.

"...but my name is really James," he said now choking up. My real name is James Roach, I'm a heroin addict and I'm tired so tired from running and hiding out with a made up name...

He went on for twenty minutes and everyone sat forward listening. When he finished saying what he could about his family dying and leaving his wife and kids, he was greeting with hugs from the group. Especially grateful for what he said was a young kid named Jerry who never knew who his father was...

Chapter XI - Justice

James feels like a weight that has been on his chest for more than three decades has finally been lifted off. Over the past three weeks, he has told more and more of his story to members of the group. His only disappointment in how his treatment worked out was he could not get into contact with Lizzy.

It seems Lizzy had left Memphis around 1979, with the boys. He was able to get in touch with Bill who seemed angry when the call was placed to him from George's office. He refused to tell James where she was.

"Are you ready to move on James?" asked George at the opening of a full group session.

"Yeah. I want to say I learned a lot about myself, and the problem I had with heroin and pain-killers. Now I am gonna go to Aftercare. I'm glad I was finally able to have let go of so much stuff I had held on to so tight."

Suddenly there is a knock on the classroom door, and the program coordinator enters.

She whispers in to George's ear and he shook his head no.

"James", he asked. "Did we do the trust thing with you?"

"The trust thing," he responded in a puzzled question kind of answer. "No, I don't think so."

Oh, man we got to do it now before we sign your papers the coordinator Gwen said.

"Every body else, leave the room. James, you sit down. Tom, you get the blindfold. Lillian you go get the rope," Wendy barked orders like a drill sergeant.

"George, man what is going on?" James asked. "I've never seen anything like this with anyone else."

"Your EAP from the Post Office sent word that on Tuesday that you have to be given the dynamic threshold of trust treatment prior to you coming back to work for them."

"What do I have to do?" James asked.

"Just trust that we can do you no harm, and that your confidentiality will be protected at all costs. Are you ready?"

"Yes."

"Remember. It's all over for you if you get the blindfold off and untie the ropes."

"Okay, with what I've been through with people who were trying to do me harm, I should be able to handle this. Let's get it over with."

For a few tense minutes there is silence, before James hears the door open and about twenty people walked in. James thought that perhaps it was a selected group of the patients.

A heavy male voice begins. "We are going to ask you questions that you must answer truthfully. If we are not satisfied we will let you know."

71

"I'm ready," James said

"What do you think your mother would say if she could see you right now?" a young woman's voice asks.

"Knowing my momma the way I did, she'd probably say how disappointed she is that I let my life turn to what it did, but that she's glad I'm getting it together."

For a few minutes there was silence. Then a young man's voice asks, "If your wife was here right now what words would you use to show you truly love her?"

Now starting to feel a little uneasy, James hesitates before answering, "I would tell her I love her in ways words could not describe"

The young girl's voice from the first question said "that's not good enough. Think that right now your wife is here with your children and grandchildren. What would you say to her to show her you love her?"

"I don't know what I'd say," James lashes out. "I feel so disappointed for not having been strong enough for her. She always seemed to know she loved me, that she cared, and I tried so hard to keep her feelings and mine separate. But once I knew I couldn't hold back anymore, I knew she would be the best thing in the world to me and for me. She bore my sons, and even gave one my real name without her knowing it. I'm so sorry, I'm so sorry I let that all get away".

There are sobs in the background and James is starting to sweat with the heat coming from the questions. A few minutes more a silence. Then he felt old hands come and wipe his brow.

Now the heavy voice begins again. "That man you stayed with, the one whose daughter you married, what would you say to him, right here right now?"

James sat silently fuming.

Then there were giggles in the background. "I think he's getting mad chuckled the voice." Then a young girl's voice said "let me ask him one."

"Not yet Shelby."

James heard a name he never heard before coming from the voice of a young man. James began to wonder who was asking him these questions.

"Who's in here?"

"We will let you know in just a minute. Before we do we want you to tell us why you've had such a hard time trusting? Why did you let your fears cause you to get up a leave two families that loved you," questions coming from a very deep voiced male.

Then an old woman's voice rings out. I just want to know one thing. "Boy, why haven't you been to church all these years?"

"Wait every body quiet. Let's take the boy to church. Yeah, let's do it"

James becomes unnerved. He doesn't recognize any voices. They are not from any part of the program that may have heard him speak, but they are asking questions about things that should have been kept confidential.

"Get me out of this chair. Get me out."

The heavy voice asks. "James, are you sure you want to do that? If you do it's all over for you. This should only take a minute more."

"Let's bring everybody back in now," he hears George's voice.

The door opens, and James hears the voices of the group members, buzzing in from the hallway.

"James, it's your choice the blindfold or the rope, which one comes off first?"

"I need to stand up. The rope first," James chose.

"Now James, before we take off the blindfold you have to relax because now I have a story for you," George said.

"When we called Mr. Davis from my office, it was the third time he was contacted. The first time was when you signed a release of information at the Post Office with your EAP. Before you came to treatment he wrote a very interesting letter back to the EAP.

In it he said he had known years ago who you really were, that he knew even at the time you lived with him. Then he called me to set this whole thing up. Is that right Bill?"

Now a gruff older man's voice with a hint of youthful laughter said "yeah, that's right. And I bet he didn't catch on to my act when we set up that last phone call."

"And Lizzy moved down to Birmingham with the boys, is that right Lizzy," the heavy voice continues the story.

"Yes, a sobbing female voice said from the group. And there I lived with a family that had this crazy member, always talking about somebody named…"

"Justice." James cried out. Sobbing he pulled the blindfold off his eyes. Looking across the crowded room his met those of a tearful woman aged about in the late forty's. Running over and through, he met her with a hug and a kiss. "I'm sorry, I'm so sorry baby. I missed you so much."

For two minutes the rest of the clients in room applauded a James and Lizzy held each other, with their eyes closed, as if the rest of the world slipped away. "Oh I missed you so much too. I dreamed this day would happen, sooner but I'm just so happy. Please let this be real."

The heavy voice male spoke, "Yo man. Don't you have something for your cousin? It's me, Lenny"

"But, I thought…." came out before being cut off.

"We all know what you thought. We all got out the house okay through the back."

"Where's…"

"Here we are," as two other men walked in the room, one a splitting image of himself. "Poppa and me are alright too. We took a beating, but we had God protecting us. We heard you went through hell in Vietnam."

"Yeah I did," whirling around quickly, then running towards his mother. "Momma this is so good…"

She hugged him hard and long rocking from side to side. "Yeah baby."

For the next five minutes James is running around crying and hugging. His aunts Angela and Pearl, sisters Gail and Margie and their husbands and children, Joseph's set of twin girls and his own two sons all take part.

"What about my question? What about my question", asked the raised voice of a young girl about five years old. "You really been lost like that Prodigal son story they tell in Sunday school grandpa?"

"Who is this little bit over here?"

"This is Shelby, your first grandchild, James' daughter," Lizzy said with her son beaming behind her. "I think she looks just like me when I was that age."

"Man, if only you all knew what I am feeling right now. I am so so very happy".

"James I hope you know there is no such thing as the trust threshold therapy. I made it up," George said.

"Man, you are too much George," one of the counselors said, probably Tom.

Then George said. "Okay every body. You know the song I want. It's the one we do before and after Role Play. And we have enough people that sing in the room I should finally get some good harmony up in here.

James Sr, you start, and your family will catch on quick enough. You all from the group can hum until the third time around, then I want the roof to come off."

The words start slowly to come out of James' mouth, softly, and choked with the tears of pain and joy. The rich baritone of both his father and twin made the chairs in the room rumble. By the time his aunt and sisters came in people from second and third floor offices were drawn in by the sound that reverberated throughout the building. And the voices of the counselors and patients joined in with the family to sing the familiar refrain.

> "Amazing Grace how sweet the sound
> that saved a wretch like me
> I once was lost but now I'm found
> Was blind but now I see..."

And as the song was sung, through all the joy and all the tears, one elderly woman sat on a soft seated rocker brought in from one of the offices just for her. And James, his family, the clients, the counselors and spectators passing by seemed treated hearing the words Angela spoke.

"Yeah. Justice been seen here today. Let me tell you bout Justice, good strong Justice ain't never did no wrong by nooo body. And finally Justice is here. Justice finally is home."

Fini

Oskar Lee

By George Langston Cook

Dedication

This story is dedicated to those who possess the knowledge of our past, and to those who have lived through it.

Introduction

The character of Oskar Lee came about as a result of a class assignment I had as a student at Arizona State University. For the class Methods of Teaching History under one Professor Phillips in 1977, I was to teach a unit at a high school in Phoenix. I had a place to practice my skills, and decided I would teach a unit on Segregation there. I wrote the lesson plan, passed out preliminary handouts to the students, and gave the Dr. Phillips the planned date for my presentation to the students. The professor came to observe that session.

Despite having received pre-knowledge handouts, the students sat there like bumps on a log, not responding to any questions on the topic. I was embarrassed and a bit frustrated, believing it was my fault the students were not responding. So in the middle of the class period, I switched tactics. Instead of asking students questions, I began telling the story of a man named Oskar Lee, born after the Civil War, and whose life mirrored the Jim Crow through the 1960's Civil Rights Eras. Before long, the students began asking me questions about what that man and his family went through. I believe they gained interest in and knowledge of the period covered.

Professor Phillips went beyond what I believe any instructor should, requesting instead of me revising the lesson plan that I write up the character and hand it in to him. I refused and received an incomplete in the course despite handing in all required work assignments. I end up with a C a year later.

Oskar Lee

Emancipation arrived and appeared as a rainbow following a heavy storm. Celebration of the Union victory fueled the passion responsible for his conception. The war had ended and Old Master returned home no longer a master. Juneteenth passed, and the Reconstruction began. On that day, Oskar Lee's birth occurred.

Hope flourished when Oskar was born, although a violent death visited the Great Emancipator. Former slaves voted and served in the State House along side with Union sympathizers instead of remaining tied to the fields. They passed laws building new schools and roads. Black and Union soldiers protected them from angry rebel veterans who came home in defeat. Old Master stayed out of sight, but allowed former slaves to remain on his land for a small fee, something all the Old Masters seemed to be doing.

Jubilation filled the air as one by one longtime illiterate ex-slave hands received Old Master's parceled off land unable to read the fine print. He opened a store and gave them the seed and tools needed to farm the land on credit. Oskar's parents Big Boy and Mammy Lee rejoiced in their good fortune without understanding the plot against them.

Old master led all the Black families into smaller and dirtier parts of the county. These areas of depleted farm land lacked water rights and civic improvements. In the towns, there were restricted to the far side of the railroad tracks. They lived in homes that were small one room shanties with dirt floors.   The called this section of town Darkietown.

The Lee family struggled to eke out a living because Old Master said he had no job to give or money to pay Big Boy during seasonal harvests. Instead, Old Master let them live off his land without paying rent. He told them of better times in the future, and they trusted him because he smiled so nice and seemed so sad.

Big Boy and Mammy talked about their firstborn learning to read and write. They sent him to the new public school when he reached age of seven instead of placing him out in the fields. They wanted him to have what they could not afford or what Old Master forbade them to have. They never learned to read themselves, nor could they understand the lessons their son now learned.

A stranger came down from the Old Union and planned to pull all the poor farmers together in one political party. He called himself a Populist. He said if all the poor farmers voted together in one block, they could fix what went wrong, and continue what had worked for so long. Old Master gave another message to poor White farmers. He said the Populist would cause the poor White farmers to lose their land the same way the Old master lost his to poor Black farmers. He stirred up hate, fear, and mistrust of the Black farmer. He ran for election against the Populist for the State Assembly.   On Election Day, Populists and Reconstruction politicians split the poor Black farmers' vote, while Old Master enjoyed the support of poor White farmers, old rebels, and other old masters.

Old Master promised the Lees and other poor Black farmers land and the tools to farm it. The Lee's felt they had nothing to lose in believing him, for as a master he never used the whip. They never heard the message he gave to poor white farmers before the election. He never openly acted bitter about how the war turned out. He always flashed a slight smile when he passed them. He mildly smiled on the day his election sent him to the State House from the Big House. He wrote new laws insuring they also had nothing to gain. The Reconstruction was over.

Then Old Master said they could not vote anymore because someone named Jim Crow created a citizenship test they could not pass, poll taxes they could not pay, and added some grandfather clauses to the voting laws. Old Master claimed he sympathized with the Lee's plight but convinced them and others to accept Jim Crow's laws.

Jim Crow's laws contributed negatively to the Darkietown atmosphere, and the old masters seemed reluctant about eliminating them. Besides being unable to vote, the Lees and their friends were unable to testify against old masters or rebel veterans in court. These laws also sent the protective Union soldiers out West to fight Indians, and many of Oskar's contemporaries joined them.

When all the crops stood ready for reaping the week before the harvest moon, hooded riders robed in white sheets descended onto all the parcels cut from Old Master's plantation and burned crosses in the field. Livestock disappeared from their pens and barns. Only the credit bill survived that onslaught. Each good farming year for ten, the pattern repeated, intermingled with bad crop years or low prices for what the farm produced.

The store soon owned the land, and Mammy and Big Boy owned a debt. They promised to work it off by farming for a small share of the profit, just enough to keep the shanty roof over their heads and feed their now burgeoning family. The Lees pulled their younger children out of school, to work the farm, practice a trade, or perform other odd labors at Old Master's house, just to make ends meet.

Mammy and Big Boy wanted Oskar to stay in school, no matter what. He obeyed his parents' wishes but cursed their ignorance and viewed Old Masters' policies more critically than his parents. His other siblings tolerated the physical labors they performed at home. They worked and played hard, talked and laughed loudly, and often joked about Oskar's studious manner.

Oskar worked in the store after completing his daily school studies. He also worked in the mill as a reward for his parents' loyalty to Old Master and his son Boss who ran the store. He received a small salary and many lectures about the evils of education from Boss. Oskar listened to Boss but noticed at the same time he damned learning, he sent his children to school daily. He kept his thoughts about the contradiction to himself, and saw boss's duplicity as a harbinger of doom.

Oskar witnessed changes in the words old masters used, as well as in their acts. They increasing called the ex-slaves "nigger, boy, coon, or darkie," instead of by their given names. They demanded that Blacks enter their homes only through a back door. They placed "Little Darkie" gaslight statues on their lawns. They talked about how darkies and niggers couldn't learn, how they hated work, drank too much liquor, and moved too slow. The only praise the old masters and rebel veterans gave the ex-slaves involved dancing, playing, singing, and praying.

Oskar also noticed that the old masters prevented their tenant farmers from making too much profit. From his vantage point in store, he saw Boss sell good meal to whites and bad meal to blacks. Boss kept two sets of credit ledgers. When a farmer he knew couldn't read came in to pay a bill, somehow a master got a credit too. Boss also restricted Oskar from making entries in either ledger.

When some disaster befell the home of an old master, the fire brigade, doctor, or sheriff responded immediately. Delays plagued answering to Darkietown emergencies, especially problems caused by the hooded riders brought fear to the black families living there. They had no recourse or means to express their grievances under Jim Crow's laws. They had midwives to attend to births, preachers to shepherd their souls, and pine boxes to bury the dead, but no means to protect themselves or their property from the riders in Darkietown. Curiously, the riders never visited an old master or rebel veteran.

The roads and schools built around the time of Oskar's birth eventually fell into disrepair. The State House controlled the money to rebuild them. Haphazard repairs occurred for those facilities servicing Darkietown residents. The old masters' children and grandchildren received new school buildings and expansive grounds. The old masters also installed paved roads, inside plumbing, and sewer systems in their portion of the county, while Darkietown resorted to using outhouses. They claimed the civic improvements and new buildings came as a result of something called a census count, which skipped over many Darkietown residents. Old Master said the two separate systems were fair to all parties concerned.

Oskar began finding black men hanging dead from trees, some with badly burned or mutilated bodies. He choked at the sight of their private parts, cut off, stuffed into their own mouths, or missing entirely. He recognized some of these men. They tried too hard to find out the identities of the hooded riders, or talked in a romantic fashion about one of Boss's daughters. Some of them were populist or other political agitators. Some of them came from the Old Union to spread the news about employment and living conditions "up North". Darkietown residents looked to these men for leadership and courage.

Oskar argued with his brother as to what would be the best course of action. He benefited from being able to read, and saw their plots up close when he worked in the store. He believed the best way to deal with the riders and way his parents were treated was to agitate and aggravate the Old Masters and their sons with legal action. He saw formal education as a means to that end. On the other hand, his brothers thought it would be a lot better to accumulate wealth within their own community. Accomplishing this goal meant perfecting practical trades and performing services.

Instead of them learning to work together on their common goals, they confused the matter with the means to get there. Old Master stirred the debate by pitting one brother against the other. One month he'd praised the dedication to education Oskar demonstrated to stroke his ego. The next month he gave Oskar's brother extra work with pay around the Big House. Oskar was too smart to see the simplicity of this plot.

Oskar hated being unable to vote. He believed everyone needed a decent education (or at least the same facilities as Boss's children). He saw his family treated like second class citizens, and they failed to make ends meet under the share the crop method of slavery. Some of the men in the family thought time to leave masters lands had come. Word passed down from the big cities in the Old Union that jobs were available, all people could vote, and you could go to the same schools and live in the same neighborhoods as the bosses' kids. The fact that the hooded riders were unheard of there also provided a great amount of motivation to leave.

Leaving Darkietown was as hard as escaping slavery on the old Underground Railroad. Old Master and his son Boss put up a lot of pressure for Oskar to stay. They told Oskar he owed them something for his education to appeal to his sense of honor. They told him his family needed him at the store to appeal to his ego. Then they hinted how difficult it may be to prevent the hooded from running roughshod over his parents' parcel once he left, to appeal to Oskar's fears. Oskar and many from his generation ignored all the urgings from Old Master and Boss, and left the Old South in droves.

Oskar planned to go to the nearest Northern urban center where he could use his formal education to obtain suitable clerical employment. He decided his family needed to stay behind until he could provide for them. He hopped onto a freight train and landed in the outskirts of Pittsburgh. He found no clerical work only back breaking, bone scarring labor in the steel mills replacing those who tried to go on strike.

The new bosses did not seem to care about where Oskar lived or how, just as long as he got there every day. They asked him no questions about the health of his family. They depended on his willingness to work long, hard hours and little else. When they found he could read and write, it became another skill they exploited to their benefit. All this made Oskar more cynical and mistrusting of the bosses. He kept himself separated from the bosses socially, who seemed to like that just fine.

Plentiful jobs did exist in the Old Union, however Oskar soon found there was a method to them as well. Many jobs, like being a porter on the railroad, a doorman, or a coachman were undesirable because there was no real salary just tips. The mills, factories, and railroads had work but more than enough people to fill them. Sometimes to get a job, the men from the country promised to give boss part of his earnings, or wait until the poor conditions at the mill caused severe injury to another worker. And sometimes the only way the men from the country would get hired was if they were breaking a strike, which often caused very bitter feelings between themselves and the European immigrants who previously held those jobs. Those bitter feelings caused riots and fights that didn't exist in the old rebels' towns.

The squalid conditions in the area Oskar lived in the Old Union were as bad as in Darkietown, and the rents were higher. The steel mills and factories seemed to own all the housing around. Gone was the nearby open land to hunt for possum, rabbit, and muskrat when times got a little hard. Land enough for small vegetable gardens to supplement the diet was hard to find as well. The steel mills owned everything, including a store where Oskar purchased every item of food and clothing. The only consolation was the nearby tavern where Oskar where Oskar quenched his daily thirst and sorrows and listened to the down home music that slowly drifted out into the neighborhood. And of course, there was always church to attend each Sunday. And just as in Darkietown, when it was time for the census count, the counters rarely showed up.

Until Oskar managed to send for some of his family, he contended with thieves breaking into his home during the day. He relied on the help of strangers until he was able to send one by one for his brothers. Together they began to save enough money to start a small family business, and made a small profit under selling the steel mill stores.

They gained respect for their effort within the neighborhood, but amongst the bosses at the steel mills, Oskar and his brothers only provided unwelcome competition. One day, the family store burned down suspiciously. Reminiscent of tactics used by the Southern hooded riders, Oskar and his brothers had no recourse but to return to the steel mills for work. Their fight for self respect, pride, recognition, and independence took on new meaning after that.

Oskar tried using the military to gain some respect and equality at home. He volunteered, went West to help tame Apache, Navaho, Comanche, and those Sioux and Blackfoot tribes that slaughtered Custer a generation before. He always fought with honor albeit without recognition that went instead to the white officers.

When the Maine was sunk in Havana's Harbor they let him engage the enemy, but gave his credit to a future president. He went to France and confronted the Hun there during the Great War. He contested his adversaries formidably. He entered every battle situation courageously, and won the day even when expected to fail. He succeeded despite lacking the trust and confidence of the officers that commanded him. They took credit for the blood he spilled. After each conflict, he returned home to find the same decrepit conditions and attitudes from which he fought to free others.

He also found his vanquished enemies taking his place in the steel mills, schools, and patronage jobs for the city while calling Oskar and his family every derogatory adjective their broken English allowed.

They bought out all the steel mills and stores, then colonized Oskar's neighborhood. They sold poor quality merchandise made by their own families. The followed Oskar and the other men from the neighborhood around in the store as if they were going to steal something. They even shot and killed one of Oskar's young nieces because they mistakenly believed the candy she ate while in the store came from off their shelf. The city administrators tried to sweep the whole matter into the background as the law was never on the side of Oskar's people.

Oskar and other veterans complained of their treatment at home, but authorities ignored their cries and warnings. Lead by veterans seeking no more than a little respect, riots broke out all over colored districts. Many people died, and no real solution arose. Cool wet weather dispersed the crowds. Oskar avoided the troubles by concentrating more on expanding his knowledge than on the material well being in comparison to others. He still believed self enlightenment would promote the progress for which he hoped.

Then, a lone voice cried out to Oskar and his contemporaries, preaching a new independence from the mind slavery war practiced by Old Master and Boss. This man Garvey's message of "Go Back to Africa" resonated throughout Darkietown. His ideas contrasted from what Oskar and his brothers promulgated, perhaps due to the foreign upbringing of this visionary. Trumped up criminal charges discredited the herald only temporarily. As this movement grew, Oskar became a willing follower.

Oskar traveled to other centers of population and culture. He sought and found new brothers of like mind, who spread the music, words, and dance originating from their parents' plantation slave quarter homes to shamelessly. Their world view and liberating expressiveness so differed from what crusty old masters, bosses, and European immigrant working classes expected. Their cultural awareness became the rage of the 1920's, was quickly copied and homogenized by profiteers, then sold to the youthful relatives of the bosses and European immigrants who no longer subscribed to the stodgy culture of their elders, save their need to remain separate and feel above the day to day lives of Oscar, his friends, and his kin and supplemented the lawless appreciation of alcohol.

A great Depression followed the lawless years where Darkietown culture was homogenized and sold to the children and relatives of Boss. Some of the old social barriers broke down as Oskar's music became the rage.

Oskar sent his leaders to petition the courts for civil equality under the law. He wanted his offspring to have the same opportunities as Boss's kids in school. He disliked public facilities not including him as part of the public. He also tired of Southern hospitality that refused to serve him at lunch counters despite his years of dedicated military service. But one of his sisters got the ball rolling when she absolutely refused to give up her bus seat to a man. Some of Old Maser's brothers balked in court, and a partial victory resulted.

Riots again rose up as progress towards goals stifled in the urban centers of the Old Union.

And at the moment agreement came on the goals and the means to get there, movement foes tarnished several reputations, vilified one part of the movement, and murdered the best and brightest. With leadership destruction completed, Oskar and his offspring had nowhere to turn for guidance. Imitators with their selfish, impure motives arose to weld the mantle of power. The movement for respect became a cry for material well being, of having what Old Master and his son Boss possessed.

The media turned on this new movement, insisting Oskar and his offspring wanted to take from the children of immigrants what their parents handed down to them. Mistrust replaced where once agreement stood. The media stroked the flames of these fears, until the immigrant working middle class backlash stunned the national leadership structure. They began taking back whatever rights and recognition once freely given, as if they belonged only to those immigrants instead of to all.

Areas of musical expertise and renown once practiced only by plantation denizens and Darkietown residents slowly became part of the public domain. First came the crisis in funding them in the public arena. Then white-washed sanitized versions began dominating the airwaves. Stolen legacies popped up as if they were new creations, and originators of beat and rhythm could not get air time. Everyone knew who controls what the media outlets puts out despite who owns that wavelength to the people.

Oskar saw a new poverty sneaking into town that no longer involved financial or material well being. It disguised itself with homelessness, hunger, and unemployment. Spurred on by a media blitz that made it all seem fine, increasing numbers of kids started engaging in frequent fornication of mind, body, and spirit, and they neglecting the good handed down from the ancients.

Finger pointing, justification, and procrastination hide their underlying selfishness. Drug use rewards them with instant gratification instead of real solutions to problems. Despite the apparent wickedness and lawlessness of their acts, they continue without regard for the future. They foolishly hold on to the myth that the life they lead will last forever, but instead they ended up incarcerated and died younger.

Now Oskar ponders the events of the day that makes up his life. The phenomena of babies making babies dominate his mind. He questions this madness, yet somehow he realizes his helplessness to stop the decay in his society was determined long ago. He knows the long range plots and plans of Old Master and Boss play a large part in the scheme of things. And Oskar questions whether the plotters possess the power to set things right before the powerful forces at work overtake them all.

AMOS

DEDICATION

I dedicate this story to a Newark that no longer exists, and to the many friends I grew up with there.

GLC

INTRODUCTION

I started writing this story about Amos thirty years ago, when I attended Essex County College in Newark, New Jersey. At the time I did not know what I wanted the story to be about, only that I wanted Amos to have a problem that he could not tell his brother about, the recent death of their father, and a friend named Buddha Walker. At the time I hand wrote maybe five pages in a notebook.

Sixteen years of substance abuse counseling have drained my spirits, so on July 1, 2005 I quit my job. I turned my back and just walked out. I became unemployed for six months, the longest period without work in my adult life. I used that time to think of what I really wanted to do with my life. I decided writing is what I wanted to return to, because it has always given me joy.

When I tore through a bag of my papers, I rediscovered my notebook, and all kinds of other little pieces of paper I had scribbled some words and thoughts on. After looking at what I had written, I made a name change to Amos' brother (don't ask), and completed what I hope you find as a nice heart warming piece.

Thank You

George Langston Cook   March 18, 2006

I

It's early February 1975 and the sun brightly lit this day as if a beautiful day in May, but the quickly falling temperature and stiff breeze in the approaching the evening hour brought the realization it was still winter. Andre strolled west along Chester Avenue in North Newark, well wrapped for the chilly weather. The rubbing sound from his corduroy pants' legs and leather soled shoed tapping against the pavement highlighted his long unmeasured steps. A black full length wool overcoat draped his tall frame and a same colored tam pulled down and forward topped the short 'fro he wore.

Andre barely noticed the coldness in wintry air or the rush of the crisply swirling gusts as they tinged the tips of his ears. Instead his gaze fell upon decaying structures dotting the lengths of local streets like ragged soldiers standing at attention immediately following a losing battle, as the sound the wind banged closed doors in their abandoned broken windowed emptiness.

He listened to the rush of cars on Broadway and other city noises. They all but drowned out the more natural sounds of young boys from around the Delavan Avenue neighborhood at play, dodging traffic while challenging a group from Triton Terrace and Peabody Place to a game of knockdown football in the street. Andre motioned to the boys for the ball that they tossed to him gladly. He pumped then tossed it down the street as two or three of the youngsters ran long to catch his pass. Then after a moment of laughter and chiding, he continued on his pensive journey.

Andre kept walking until he reached his destination, a small store fronted building near the corner of Broadway and Delavan Avenue. Etched on the large pane glass window shuttered by rusting security bars was the likeness of the Christ crucifixion. Above the window a hand painted wooden sign hung with bailing wire read, "The Holy Name of Jesus Pentecostal Church-All are Welcome." Andre paused outside the door, smoking a cigarette while thinking of the circumstances bringing him to this place.

A few days earlier, Andre was away at Norfolk State, playing basketball on its team and was its leading scorer. Everything was looking good for his future until he received word of his father's death. He rushed home to find even more bad news. Andre's older brother, Amos, seemed to be struggling with living. The superstition about death occurring in threes made people believe he would be the next in the family to die mostly because of the strange things he had been doing of late.

Amos had quit his job and given up his luxurious apartment right after Andre left for school in mid August. He moved in with his estranged father, "Big Henry", over the next several months but left there right after his papasan had unexpectantly entered a coma. He then holed himself up in his old bedroom at his mother's apartment in the Grafton Avenue projects. Without speaking the word itself, Amos' mother Miss Dot and some other family members hinted their belief Amos was on the verge of committing suicide.

After trying to talk to Amos in the days since coming home, Andre grudgingly agreed with his mama that something was wrong the brother he had looked up to for years. He decided to seek advice from an old friend of Amos, the Reverend Buddha Walker.

Andre put out his smoke before entering the door of the building. The church had no pews or a sacrificial altar in the conventional sense. Grey folding chairs appearing to be as frail as the crumbling neighborhood outside littered the fringes of the small hall, while some second hand kitchen chairs, bean bags, and stacks of large pillows filled the interior space. A wooden podium that looked salvaged from a junkyard having two pieces of wood nailed on it to form a cross stood on a slightly raised section of the floor in front of the ragged conglomeration of seating. Behind the podium, painted on a wood panel hanging on the wall was another sign reading, "This is God's House, Make Yourself at Home."

After casually eye balling the space and side stepping the seating, Andre made his way to an open door in the side of the room. A small office about the size of a jail cell was situated on the other side of the door. Sitting on a cloth covered swivel chair, working at a desk was Reverend Walker. As Andre entered the office, Buddha turned around nimbly to see who came in.

"Well, God bless my soul. If it isn't my man Andre, the answer to Walt Frazier in the flesh. It's good to see you, boy" boomed Buddha in a voice that nearly startled Andre. He jumped up from his seat and flung himself open armed towards Andre like a child flies to a Christmas tree after too long of a Christmas Eve sleep.

"Give me five" he said as he reached out his hand for the customary salute.

Andre shook the big hand of the preacher man who returned the greeting with a bear hug lifting him nearly a foot off the floor.

"Yeah. It's good to see you too, Buddha. How's the family doing?" Andre asks.

"Everybody is alright on this end," Buddha says. "My brother opened a small business in Atlanta and my sister just had her third son. I heard about your pops, man. You handling it alright?"

"Yeah, I'm okay but you know Momma ain't taking it so good."

"You'd figure after all those years they been apart, what is it eight now, that she would have gotten over the old dawg, beggin' my pardon Sir Dre."

"No problem. Pops was definitely getting' his, but you know my momma is one of those old fashioned country girls, one man only for her. If she gonna do anything, she may go upstairs for a little nip of gin with Miss Julia."

"Yeah Miss Dot was always different from the other women in the bricks. You know I will keep yo fam'ly in my prayers, Dre"

"I see you're still playing," Andre says looking towards the desk and spying an unhinged tenor saxophone case underneath it.

"Yeah, I play some in church here. Blowing a little wind through that old Whistler there makes my sermons…well…different. Sometimes I don't have to say a word, and the music raises the Spirit in the congregation"

The preacher sat down and ushered Andre to the only other seat in the tiny office. After pausing a few seconds, he asked about Amos. "What has the A-man been up to? He hasn't been coming around here much lately, and I haven't seen him at any of our mutual haunts."

"That's what I came to see you about. No one really seems to know what's going on with him," Andre said.

"What's up with him?" quizzed Buddha.

"Well, I really wasn't here when all this fuss with him started. It happened after I left for school six months ago. Before that he seemed okay and enjoyed himself in so many ways. He did say he had something to talk to Pops about before I left, but he didn't tell me what it was about.

Since then he changed a lot as if something happened to him. He's been acting kind of strange and everyone is worried he might hurt himself. No body understands him anymore, and he does not seem to be givin' us a chance to. We all would appreciate it if you go speak to him if you can."

Andre lowered his hands from his cheeks where they had been since he sat down. He looked around the small cluttered office for something to take his mind what he was doing there. His eyes latched on to the picture of the Last Supper. He focused on the glowing halos that adorned the heads of all the characters. He caught a slight shiver as he thought about Judas and what he was soon to do also having an aura about him. He felt in a way he was betraying his brother who had told him not to worry and that everything was all right. Andre wondered if Amos would call him a Judas.

The reverend was a patient man, and he waited while Andre looked around. After a moment Andre turns to him again.

"Well, I don't know. I know your brother too. Remember we went to school together when you were still wearing short pants. What do you think 's up with him?"

"He don't seem to want to live anymore. He skips a lot of meals and his clothes are starting to fit on him kind of loose and ragged. He's lost a lot of weight, Buddha" Andre said.

"Are you sure he ain't on drugs or somethin' like that. Even though he never did that stuff when we were running together, it seems so many of the old guard are dippin' and dappin' now. Maybe he just fell in love again. Remember the changes he went through behind…you know…what's her name, that Rogers girl? Yeah, Sheila."

Andre answers Buddha with a sense of knowing, "It's not love because he ain't gone out the house to see anyone or made any phone calls. And it can't be dope, because none of the dealers can get into my momma's house where he's been holed up in his old bedroom for the past few days without them getting' bashed in the head with her rollin' pin. This is somethin' different, beyond any woman or drug. That's why I came to you. You and Amos always had a special way of getting' through to each other. Remember how he broke that funk you were in when you first got back from the Nam? Maybe you might be able to find out what's goin' on with him, find out what's on his mind."

"Me and the A-man have been through some close calls and hung out together for a lot of years, man. We've been through a whole lot together. You know… I'll do anythin' I can to help. He's at your momma's house now? Let me wrap up a few things and we'll go over there.

Buddha shuffles some papers into a pile on his desk, then reaches down to snap the case of his sax closed. "You never know how the Lord will provide an answer to this, but just have faith he will," he said as he picked up his instrument.

Then, the two men got up, locked up the church door, and walked toward the red brick high rise projects near the river.

II

It's the late part of August in 1974, and Amos is walking with his younger brother Andre the few short blocks down Raymond Boulevard from Broad Street towards the Greyhound bus station in Newark's Penn Station. Andre received a college basketball scholarship and is on his way register and attend fall classes at Norfolk State for the first time. Amos volunteered to buy the bus ticket and help with his brother's luggage really more as an excuse to spend some parting moments with him.

They engaged in some loud light-hearted brotherly banter during the stroll.

"Yo bro, I'm gonna miss you. It sure's gonna be a lot more quiet in Newark with you in Norfolk," Amos teased. "Man I don't know how you got that scholarship with your no jump shot shooting behind self."

"You just jealous because you got no game at all, you wanna be bench warming scrug you. And maybe you might be able to get a little some-some too, now that I won't be here," Andre responded gleefully, occasionally throwing a light jab at Amos shoulder.

As they got closer to the station the talk got a little more serious and the volume toned down.

"No, really man. Take care of yourself. College has good and bad points just like here in Newark. I know you can make it Andre."

"Yeah A-man I will. Don't forget to look in on Moms and Pops for me. Just because you up in Ivy Hill now don't mean you can't come down bottom any more."

"Yeah, I will. I got something I got to talk over with Pops anyway."

"Like what Amos."

"Grown folk talk is all you gotta know about it now," Amos teased for a moment then he said "I've been thinking about somethin' for a while that's kind of important to me and I jus' wanna bounce it off Pops. Maybe I'll write you about it after you get settled into school.

"Here you go sounding all mysterious and stuff. What you done gone and did, make a baby or did you fall in love again?"

"Nah man, it ain't nothing like that."

"Well okay big brother. Just make sure you keep in touch whatever it is. And keep track of my scoring down there too. I'll send clippings."

Arriving at the station, Amos goes to the ticket counter and lays down the thirty seven dollars and change for the round trip ticket. He returns to Andre who is waiting for the ticket just outside the door so he could check his luggage.

"Look, while you're in Norfolk, don't forget to look up Momma's people. If nothing else Aunt Mary got that soft as hell bed upstairs, if the cot at the school gets a bit hard. You know she always plays church music in the house, but it's cozy there. Or you can go over to Aunt Dot's and Uncle Will's house. It may be more to your liking because Pearl and Stella got girlfriends they can introduce you to if you strike out on campus."

"A-man, you know...."

"Yeah I do. Keep it covered bro. Since you gonna be big man on campus be careful or one of those North Carolina honeys will have you in a shotgun wedding if you're not."

"All aboard", yells the bus driver as he starts checking tickets at the door. Amos opens his arms to give a farewell hug to his brother. After they break the hug, Amos throws a quick hard jab to his chest.

"And don't forget what I taught you, you bum," he laughed as the punch caught Andre off guard.

"Okay bro. I'll write. You take it easy," Andre said getting on the bus.

Seated by the window near the back of the bus, Andre looked towards his brother waving as the bus pulled off. He wondered what it was that his brother could find so important that he had to talk to his father about, and so secret that he could not tell him.

III

It's mid August 1974. Two men, father and son open the door and walk into Sophie's restaurant, a small greasy spoon diner on Broadway near Bloomfield Avenue. Inside there is an L shaped counter with seating for six and five tables around which four can eat in close proximity to each other. Sophie's does mostly a sit down breakfast and lunch take-out business, and the space for seating is a premium in this old, Italian neighborhood.

Amos walks to the counter with Big Henry where they order breakfast plates.

"Nick, I want the home fries instead of grits, and give me beef bacon. Amos orders before asking, "You got it, right?"

"Yeah we got it," the Greek owner and counter replies. "You want toast and coffee? How you want those eggs?"

"Coffee and toast sound good, scramble them eggs with cheese. Then Amos walks over to one of the few tables while his father Henry orders then joins him.

"Yeah it's good to see you son. What brings you down here this early in the morning?"

Amos began. "I think I'm gonna quit my job."

"And why do you wanna go do something like that, son. Who will you be able to count on for cash?"

"Well Pops, I've been thinking of a lot lately. Things are going good for me on the job. I got a nice little place. I'm saving a few dollars here and there. If I left well enough alone, everything would be all right. But I'm not happy with what I'm doing with myself"

"Why not Amos?"

"I'm not sure, really. I just get the feeling sometimes that I should be doing something else, something that's more about me than shuffling papers. I think I got something to say, something special, but I can't get to it because of the clutter of my life. I could use a little advice, and since everyone says we're so much alike, I figured I'd ask you."

Both men pause in their conversation for a moment as they go to the counter for their plates. They take small nibbles out of each item on their platter before continuing.

"I understand. You have to follow your heart. But you know that. I told you that part before. What is really the problem?"

"It's not so much the about giving up the job security. It's about how am I going to get into myself, how am I gonna find that voice through all the clutter. I'm still not sure enough about myself to go for it."

"Damn. If you're scared, prayer and meditation will help. And if you can't hear yourself think maybe fasting will help too. You saw what that fast did for Dick Gregory didn't you?"

"Yeah, he fasted for what, 5 years. I hope I don't have to go through something like that."

"By the way, did I ever tell you how I got to marry your mother?" Big Henry asks.

"No not really. All I know is that you both were in the service, met there on some base, and got married near the end of the war."

"There was more to it than that though. I had a son, your brother Butch before I went into the Army. Even though I wasn't married to his momma, I thought when I got out, I would move back to Paterson and be with them. Then I met your mother when I was stationed in Walla Walla."

"Yeah, I remember you telling me a little something about meeting Momma. She still doesn't talk about it much."

"Dot was different from all those girls I use to know from the city, nice and sweet and to tell you the truth, I didn't know how to speak to her. And it wasn't one of those things you talk over with your buddies, and my father had long since passed on."

"But about eight months before the end of the war I started fasting and praying on it. I mean I got really sick over it, and the doctors at sick call tried to figure out what was going on with me. The funny thing is that I felt alright but it did not look like it to anyone besides me."

"Momma had you like that? You mean you had a love jones Pop. What was it, love at first sight huh?

"No it wasn't like that. I was out of it, I mean everyone even Dot thought I would die. I'm not even sure how much of that time I was really conscious."

"It sounds like you had it bad, but I been there Pops."

"I barely ate, and after standing my duties everyday, I spent all my time in my rack reading out of the Bible. I lost weight, damn I lost a stripe too because more than a few times an officer thought I was being insubordinate."

"I know what that part feels like Pops. I know sometimes my supervisors think I like going over their heads with my ideas, but their bosses like my contributions."

It took a few months to pull out of it and all I can tell you is that when I came to, I was able to find words to express myself in a way that I never knew possible. I used that time to look inside myself, and was able to ask your mother to marry me when it was over."

"How did you come out of it?"

"I'm not sure of how I got in it, and I think only by the grace of God did I get through it."

"So you're telling me that if I look inside myself I'll find what I'm trying to get out?"

"What I'm saying is that if your search is anything like mine, I would love to be there to hear what comes out of you."

"You'll be there Pops, and I'll do it special just for you."

"I'd like that a lot."

"Anytime Pops, anytime."

"By the way Amos, when I was sick the way I was back then, it worried your mother so much, she lost some of her hair, it just fell out. Just because she worries so much, I still try not to put too much to her, even though we're not married anymore.

She knows about my heart condition because I was at home when I had my first heart attack. She knows about my diabetes because I keep an emergency supply of insulin there, just in case I stop over.

What she doesn't know is that I have cancer in my stomach. It's inoperable."

Amos looked at his father shocked and bewildered over the revelation. "What are you talking about Pops?"

"I am dying, and outside of my doctor, me, and now you, nobody knows, and I would like it to stay that way. I wasn't given more six months to live. And I do not want you to tell anyone until it's over for me."

For a tense moment, there was nothing but silence between the two men. Amos was in shock, not knowing what to say, and unable to grasp what it was he was feeling. He looked carefully at his father now seeing for the first time since they sat to eat worry lines etched onto his elder's face.

After what seemed like an eternity to him, Amos spoke. "Pops," Amos blurted "man this hurts. It just ain't right. Just when I thought we was getting' closer. Why this mess gotta happen now?"

Seeing the concern in his son's expression and hearing it in his voice, Big Henry added, "Look Amos, I made peace with the man over this, so I'm okay with it. I'm sorry I broke it down to you like this but I wasn't gonna say anything at first. I just thought if I could trust anyone with this, it was you. I just hope you can keep it to yourself for now."

"You mean not even to tell Andre? You know he's going off to school in a little more than a week. You know it's gonna be hard for me not to tell him."

"Yeah especially don't tell your brother. The last thing I want is him fretting over what he can't change. And since he is going off to school he doesn't need any distractions. He's the first in the fam'ly to get that chance at college. So please, tell no one 'bout this thing I got, absolutely no one. You gotta promise me before you leave out of here today. Can I trust you to do that for me?"

"If that's what you want from me you got it. Would it be okay if I come by to check on you and spend some time with you?"

"Yeah Amos. I would like that a lot. There is so much I want to tell you before my time. In fact why don't you just move in unless you can't handle me being sick."

"I think I can handle it Pops."

Amos and Big Henry quietly finish their meal. Before getting up from the table Amos makes the promise to his father to keep the secret from everyone. He also made a promise to himself that his first performance would be for his father.

IV

Andy and Buddha walk into Miss Dot's house right in time for dinner. Greeting and being greeted with warms hugs and where have you been, he sat down with the rest of the family at the table. On his plate sat baked chicken, macaroni and cheese, collard greens, and a piece of cornbread.

"I hope you aren't one of those that don't eat pork anymore because you know that's how I fix my greens," Andy's mother said. "Buddha, you say grace for us please."

"Miss Dot, you know I ain't never turned down even one of your plates, and yes I still eat pork. Please now, let us bow our heads and touch hands."

Then Buddha gave a blessing for the home, the table, and each person. "Amen."

"Amen," was the chorus from the table before everyone began eating. After twenty minutes of food, laughter, and small talk, the conversation turned to Amos.

"Where is he at Miss Dot?"

"He's in the middle bedroom," she said as a tear welled up in her eyes. "Please talk to him for us, for me. I am so worried. I just lost the kid's father, and I don't know what I'd do if I had to lose one of them too."

"I'll go do that right away, Miss Dot," he said rising up from the table.

"Take him something to eat please. He hasn't been out the room all day except to do his business in the bathroom. I ain't seen him eat anything since yesterday afternoon."

Okay. Just give me a piece of cornbread on a saucer. I know how much he loves your cornbread. I'll get him to eat at least that and drink some Kool-Aid.

Buddha picks up his Sax case and heads to the middle bedroom door. Stopping at the entrance, he knocks three quick raps then two slow ones.

Through the door he hears the voice of his friend. "That's either Buddha or the devil pretending to be him, and the devil ain't that bad.

"Yeah, he thought he was but I got too much of the Lord with me," Buddha responded as if answering the call sign of a secret society.

"Man get in here. I knew it would only be a matter of time before you showed up here."

Buddha opens the door and walks in. Sitting half dressed on the bed in a sloppily kept room was Amos. Buddha's eyes take in Amos' physical condition, noticing an obvious loss of weight from his six foot frame. Once about the size of a small linebacker, Amos looked skinny like his body now only carried the stature of a middle-weight boxer.

"Man. What is up with you and that weight loss thing", Buddha asks as he closes the door behind him entering the room.

"What ever happened to how are you, its good to see ya, Buddha?" Amos said as he gets up and greets his friend with their special dap. "I'm okay and it's good to see you too, bro. See you got the old whizzer with you."

"Like I asked A-man, what's up with you? Man I can see why you got everyone worried. You look like you are just wasting away."

"Now don't you go and start doing that yo momma is worried stuff on me preacher man. Ya gotta trust me that I'm alright," Amos retorted. "If you remember, it was me who wouldn't ever play chicken when we were kids and I ain't gonna start now."

"Okay…okay. Let's just talk then. Why you been hiding up here at yo momma's house? Last we spoke you had a nice little place up on Clinton Hill," Buddha responds.

"I gave that place up, and my getting lean got a purpose too. I would have thought you of all people would know I don't do nothing that don't mean something."

"I would have thought so too, but looking around and seeing this kinda reminds me of the way I got when I came back to the world."

"Nah, man. It's nothing like that."

Well, who is she? What woman done got your nose open that wide for you to go change the way you livin'," Buddha asks laughingly.

"It ain't that either."

"Then what you been doing holed up in this bedroom barely coming out to eat or wash up for the last six weeks. Yo little brother thinks you done gone crazy, and yo momma thinking you about to die. And me I don't know what to think. So if you got a plan, now is the time to let me in on it."

He walked to the dresser and reached for the tattered book on its top. He turned to a couple of dog eared pages and showed them to Buddha.

"Divine inspiration, huh?"

"You the only one I thought would understand," said Amos. "I've been really busy up in this piece.

Before I quit the job and gave up my place, I thought a lot about the days we had that little band. I loved music then. There wasn't any money in it for us then, but it was good work. Then you got drafted, and it all fell apart. Since my lottery number didn't come up I had to find a jay oh bee to get over. It was more of a slave thing, if you can dig what I'm saying.

My life was too busy and I wasn't happy doing everything I was doing. I mean the work was good and so was the pay, but it just wasn't me anymore. So I just got up and left it. I came here to cut my expenses and to be safe. I knew I could not do what I needed to do out there, and keep safe at the same time."

"And so you jump from the frying pan into the fire. You know this book said faith without works is dead, that you have to be practical about living."

"Stop it preacher. I ain't jokin' about this."

Buddha asks, "Well why didn't you tell Miss Dot, why didn't you tell someone what you were doin' Amos?"

"I did. I told my Pops when he told me about his cancer. He knew what I had to do. In fact he helped me out by tellin' me about what made him marry my Moms thirty years ago. You know I was livin with him and helping him out too until he went into the coma."

"Yeah I'm sorry about your loss man", Buddha intimated. "I didn't know he was that sick until he passed on Saturday. When is the wake?"

"Tomorrow, and the funeral is the day after at his church. You know, before I started staying up here I spent a lotta time talking with him. He told me how for almost six months he acted like he was sick, fasting, and seeing things different after a few months. He told me about how his visions lead him in the right direction."

"After not eatin' right for six months, I would be having visions, too", Buddha quipped.

"Stop jiggin' with me Buddha. There is something else you gotta know about this."

Amos stood up from his seat again, bends down and reaches under the bed for a satchel, overflowing with paper. He pulls out three sheets from the middle of the bag and hands them to Buddha.

"Take a look at this. It's for the wake tomorrow."

Buddha sits down in a recliner between the bed and the window and peruses over the ink splotches on the pages.

"Man…this looks pretty good. Why you got to come up here and be like this to do something that good? Buddha asks with a touch of amazement.

"Look preacher, you are looking at the fruit of my labor. I just could not hear the voice living the way I was. I did what I had to. Do you want to try it."

"Yeah," Buddha said. Then he asked, "You still got your horn? You got enough wind left in you to get that sound you use to have? How are your chops?"

Amos reaches under his bed again, this time pulling out a case for a trombone. "Man I thought you would never ask. My part is a lot different from yours though." he said as he pulls a few more sheets from the satchel. "The way I wrote this all the melodies are different, but watch what happens when we blow this thing together."

Amos throws his case on the bed, opens it up, and takes out a silver tone trombone. He assembles the bell to the slide and attaches the mouthpiece. He put his lips over the mouthpiece and blew air through the horn, while opening the spit valve at the far end of the slide. Then he began vibrating his lips in the cup of the mouthpiece, while pushing air up from his diaphragm.

At the same time, Buddha takes his mouthpiece out, mouths his reed before attaching it to the ebony part. Then he attaches it to the neck of his horn. He hooks his instrument a neck strap and begins blowing long tones through the mouthpiece to warm up and tune the sax.

The two men looked at each other for a moment, ascertaining they were ready to play. "You do your part first, preacher man." Amos told Buddha.

Buddha started playing the music written on the page. "Take a little bit slower, man. This ain't a march or rock n' roll." And Buddha responds to the instruction.

"Yeah," he said as he finished going through the piece one time. "This almost feels as good as making love. This is really nice."

Outside the door in the living room, all the idle discussion stops, and Miss Dot walks over to the television and turns it off. Andre gets off the couch and walks close to the middle bedroom door.

"Now listen to my part," said Amos, and he begins playing his horn. The song sounded different but similar to what Buddha had played just a minute before.

"Man, that is sweeeeet!!!" Buddha raises his voice. "So this is it? This is why you been here locked up in this room for the last few?"

"Yep, since my pops went into his coma." Then Amos asks, You ready to do it together man?"

"Yeah, let's do this."

"Here's to you Pops said Amos before counting off to the beginning.

"Thank you, Jesus" replied Buddha.

As the two men began playing, the ears in Miss Dot's could focus on nothing else. Tears welled up then fell from the eyes of the woman who had days before lost her ex-husband at the sounds she heard coming from the room.

The expression on Andre's face changed from alarm and concern to joy, as he raised both fists in the air in celebration, as if he just scored the game winning basket with a only tick left on the clock. "Yes!" he shouted.

And Miss Dot cries openly in the front room. "Yes. Thank you Lord, Jesus. Everything is gonna be alright."

Fini

Gee

Gee lived in urban America. His surrounding accented his poverty. Despite his indigence, visions called upon him regularly. He saw beyond the horizon and past the clouds. God touched him and blessed him with the gift of prophecy. Despite his gift Gee maintained a sense of humility.

He spoke softly, but no one really listened. They judged him by his appearance and belittled his existence. They called him crazy and ignored his assertions. They claimed he lacked proper credentials. When his words came to pass, they attributed them to another. Gee loved everyone regardless of them kicking him around.

Gee once prophesized that a particular day would come when people realized his true importance in the scheme of all things. He spoke of it often and anticipated this day for as long as anyone can remember, and then finally, it arrived.

People were blind to what the day had to bring. Its dawn hid behind fog, invisible to all human eyes. As the fog moved, it swirled around hot electric lights and small oil lamps alike, but yet still failed to shed onto the senses of ordinary men wonders of the sun. Gee saw through the haze.

It started slowly at first. The fog rose as if a heavy pressure needed to release itself, or as if the hand of God lifted it. Each second it gained altitude. Before long, commoners grappled to understand what the day had to offer. Gee knew what others barely imagined.

Towards the eastern horizon, the gray colored earth gave way to a sky painted in the richest of blues. Small puffy clouds sparsely embedded within the blue hid a tint of silver on their far away side. The sky brightened, its colors lightened preparing each ones gaze for the inevitable. Gee felt the coming.

Then the sun showed itself. It projected a warming yellow glow that lit up everywhere it touched. At the very moment light landed on the face of the world and cast out the darkness, Gee took the hand of God and left everyone to ponder their fate without his aid.

Drunken Stupor

Old man Bob wearily pulled himself up the last stair before reaching his doorway. While fumbling for his keys, he thought only of falling onto his bed, sleeping, and forgetting about it all until tomorrow. "Never again", he mumbled to himself. Never again would he drink one more at the urgings of whoever they were. He finally succeeded in opening the apartment door, stumbled into the empty darkened living room, and dropped onto the couch in his drunken stupor.

His head spun following a disagreement with the boss, and his spirits drooped after consuming a few too many drinks at the local tavern afterwards. Lackluster performances and self pity highlighted the predominant thoughts surrounding his activities. Declining physical functioning fed his fears. He looked into mirrors and hated what he saw, then blamed God for making him that way. This had become his daily routine over the last few years since his wife died. He lacked any will to change the direction his life was going.

Images and ideas revolved around his head chaotically, and each thought refused to stay put. He fought to gain control of his senses by focusing on a light filtering through a window. His concentration lasted only a few minutes, as the light itself began rotating. Bob tossed and turned to find a position where the universe stopped moving. He grasped hold of the couch tightly as if the motion he detected would throw him off into oblivion, regardless of what else he tried. A nasty, bubbling, bitter tasting feeling heaved up from the pit of his stomach. He fought to keep its heavy presence down in his gut. He believed he had it all under control and shut off, but after a short time, it kept burning its way up through his gullet again. He tried to cool off, thinking the infernal heat inside of him was the culprit, but cold compresses and the wintry air bludgeoning him from broken windows failed to abate the feeling. Even the bucket he kept nearby for such emergencies was out of reach. A thick, greenish-yellow, foul smelling ooze exploded out of his quivering sweat wrenched body and formed a pool, half on the couch and half on the floor.

Nothing worked for him, until he rolled off the couch, crumpling to the floor into a deep, deep, sleep. In his near comatose state, Bob dreamt of humble beginnings, grandiose expectations, and an empty present.

Buy My Book

my lights will be off by the end of this week
sugar water and rice is all that I have to eat
I'm down to my last penny and I haven't a job
But I'm not the person that you I will rob

Instead I'm up early before morning light
And begin the routine to help me write
I spend the day writing short stories and rhyme
Hoping that my creations stand the test of time

But it won't really matter what I'm tryin' to do
If they shut off my power for my bills that are due
So I'm putting this out there to perhaps catch an eye
And maybe my product you'll be willing to buy

So please take the time and be willing to look
And if your heart's willing please buy my book

About the Author

George Langston Cook was born May 23, 1952 in Newark, New Jersey to George Henry and Lucy Mae Langston Cook. The third child and oldest son of this marriage's seven children, George was raised in the federal housing projects of Christopher Columbus Homes, and educated in Newark's public schools.

After graduating high school he entered the U.S. Navy during the Vietnam Era, where he began to photograph and write for his own pleasure. Upon his Honorable Discharge in 1974, George enrolled in Essex County College in Newark where earned an Associates Degree in Secondary Education. He gained some notoriety with his participation in student publication activities and before graduating with honors. He continued his education and student activities at Arizona State University, where he received his Bachelors of Science degree in History, and became a member of Alpha Phi Alpha Fraternity, Inc.

Mr. Cook has spent most of the last 25 years employed in Social Services, as a Teacher or a Substance Abuse Counselor in both Newark New Jersey and Phoenix Arizona. He has continued writing over that period.